THE WAY WE BURN

J.D. FONDRY

Editor: Emily A. Lawrence of Lawrence Editing
Cover Design & Interior Formatting: Qamber Designs & Media
Cover photo: Shutterstock
Headshot by Éva Watson

"The only people for me are the mad ones, the ones who are mad to live, mad to talk, mad to be saved, desirous of everything at the same time, the ones who never yawn or say a commonplace thing, but burn, burn, burn like fabulous yellow roman candles exploding like spiders across the stars."

— Jack Kerouac

THE WAY WE BURN PLAYLIST:

Sound of Madness – Shinedown
Living Dead Girl – Rob Zombie
Swalla – Jason Derulo
Here We Go – P.O.D
Adrenalize – In This Moment
KILL4ME – Marilyn Manson
Over Now – Post Malone
Huggin' & Kissin' – Big Black Delta
Bittersweet – Fuel
There's No Way – Lauv
Return of The Mack – Mark Morrison
I Like Me Better - Lauv
Big Bad Wolf – In This Moment
Scars – Basement Jaxx
Flagpole Sitta – Harvey Danger
Everyday – Ariana Grande
LOCO – Machine Gun Kelly
If I Could Fall in Love – Lenny Kravitz
What Ifs – Kane Brown
Lovers –Anna of the North
Timber – Pitbull
Blurry – Puddle of Mud
Wasting My Time – Default
Halsey—Without Me

CHAPTER ONE

PALMER

"FUCK!" THE SUDDEN BLARE OF a horn causes me to jump out of my skin, bashing my head on the underside of the car I'm working on. I wince as I cradle the throbbing lump that's already forming. Looking up, I see Travis' wolfish grin leering at me through the windshield. He chuckles, knowing he startled me. I reach over to turn down the stereo as "Sound of Madness" by Shinedown blares through the surround sound.

"You're a real pain in my ass, you know that? Remind me to beat you after I'm done being concussed."

"Oh, quit being such a pussy. You're fine, and hurry up, will ya? I'm starving and I wanna get to Buckey's before the crowd of college students gets there and takes all the good seats."

I'm not entirely sure what criteria seats at an establishment like Buckey's needs to meet to be considered *good*, but I'm sure if you ask Trav, he'll tell you. In great detail, and then *never stop talking*.

Travis Palmer, my nephew; good kid, but a total chatterbox, that one. Who could blame him, though? He needs someone to talk to since his home life is a joke. His poor excuse for a father skipped out about eight years ago and left my older sister, Jamie, to be a single parent. Since then I've been helping wherever I can, including giving Travis a part-time job at my auto shop. Keeps him out of trouble and I'm hoping to teach him how to make an honest living so down the road if he decides to have kids, he won't flake out like his sperm donor of a father. The cycle repeating itself and all that. So as much as I want to pull my hair out half the time, he really is a good kid. With the students from the surrounding colleges home on break, I know he's itching to get out and stir up some trouble—I'll be damned if I didn't do the same at his age.

"How the hell are you about to call me a pussy when you're the one complaining about some damn seats at the local dive?" I throw the hand towel from my back pocket at his face. He doesn't even attempt to duck and it hits him square between the eyes.

Bull's-eye.

Buckey's isn't a bad spot to hang out by any means. It's your average local hot spot in a small town. It borders a few schools in the area, so it's usually overrun with hotshot frat boys and their stuck-up girlfriends—or fuck boys and thots, as Travis will tell you—but I have no fucking clue what either of those mean. Toss in a few of the local drunk, overweight baby boomers and you have yourselves a typical Saturday summer night in our town.

Beacon Hill, New York; it ain't much, but it's home.

"Yeah, yeah…clean up and let's *go*. I heard from a few people that there's a new bartender in town. She's supposed to be a babe, and I would like to decide that for myself and I can only do that if you get. Your. Self. In. Gear." Travis punctuates each syllable with alternating soft punches to my chest. Winding up, I sock him straight in the arm and he winces, covering the freshly pounded flesh with his other hand.

"Careful, Uncle Cole, wouldn't wanna break something in your old age, now would ya?"

I'm thirty-six. That's hardly geriatric.

Kid is always giving me shit about being an old man. "And scrub that trademark pretty face of yours so I'm less embarrassed to be seen with you in public." He takes off before I can smack him again.

I can't even help but laugh—he's such a strange kid sometimes. Although he does have a point and I really do need to wash up. I can't get my first look at the new girl in town with dirty clothes and a grease-covered face. The rest of the town already looks at me with disdain. I might as well attempt to make a good impression.

"Planned on swinging by the house first anyway. I'll clean up, then we'll get you some damn food, a cold drink, and some eye candy."

This day is about to get a whole lot better.

Kennedy

THIS DAY COULD NOT GET *any worse.*

I sweep up the shards of broken glass mocking me from the floor. So far today I've dropped two shaker pints, sliced my finger while cutting up garnishes, and even managed to drop a box on my boss's head.

Absolutely killing your first day, Kenj. That's the way to keep a job!

Fortunately for me, my boss is my uncle. Jim is about as close to a father figure as I've ever had. My actual father left my mom when she was pregnant with me and my twin brother, moving halfway across the country with some woman named Janice. Jane? Jillian?—Who knows. A woman who was *not* my mother, and I haven't heard from him since. My mom is a drunk, with a capital *D*. The woman barely kept her mouth off the bottle long enough to have us, and it got worse once we were born. Or so I'm told. Now she gets her kicks mooching off her current boyfriend, who owns half of Illinois. She moved out that way from Massachusetts to live with him a few years ago after...*everything*. She couldn't cope with the tragedy that hit our family. Since then, her new meal ticket keeps her liquored up and her pockets full, and I keep my nose out of their business. Uncle Jim would always pop in occasionally while we were growing up to check on us, making sure we were being fed, bathed, and hopefully still breathing. Until of course my mom came into enough money that she could hire a full-time nanny to *mother* us.

*Un*fortunately for me, I need this job. I have to save up to take more courses next semester to keep me on track with my degree and those bad boys aren't cheap. Not to be all *woe is me*, but money is a touchy subject right now. We grew up with money since my mother's preferred type seems to be rich; but since said parent, note *singular*, doesn't know how to actually be a parent, I've since had to pave my own way. When my mom's half-brother Jim offered for me to wait tables and mix a few drinks at his bar, I quite literally couldn't turn down the offer.

"Kenny girl, can you go turn the music on for me, hon?

I forgot to when I came in today. Nothing that makes my ears bleed, though...I've heard your music selection. I want people to stay and drink, not run screaming for the hills." He gives me a wink as he traipses toward his office in the back of the bar.

"Sure thing, boss man." I stick my tongue out at the back of his retreating figure and make my way to the updated Jukebox system behind me.

I hit the power button and shift through the pages. Within seconds, "Living Dead Girl" by Rob Zombie oozes from the speakers and I wait for Jim's reaction with a grin plastered on my face. His deep brown irises find my hazel ones from across the room and he simply shakes his head, continuing toward his desk, never once uttering a single word. I skip my way through the partition between the bar and the seating area and groove along to the music while I wipe down tables and make sure everything is in order. Jim gave me the rundown of this place, and I know the regulars and students from the few surrounding schools will be in soon, so I want to make sure I have places for people to sit while I get ready for my first shift.

PALMER

IT'S ALMOST FIVE THIRTY WHEN we arrive at Buckey's, and there aren't many other cars in the parking lot.

So much for losing your good seats, Trav.

It tends to be slower throughout the day on weekdays

anyway—then this place really gets rockin' on the weekend. The owner of the bar, Jim Buckey, always lets people come in and grab a seat early. He's good people and loved by pretty much everyone in our little town. Thankfully, he's always been a decent guy and has never held my past over my head, unlike everyone else in the area.

Travis and I scramble through the main door, causing the bell overhead to chime. I find myself laughing at something idiotic he's yammering on about. As usual.

The first thing I notice as I walk in is that the music selection is...different.

Way to go, Jimmy boy, finally getting some good tunes in this place.

The second thing I notice is the group of college-aged guys congregated at the pool tables, whispering amongst themselves and staring across the room. I follow their gazes, which land behind the bar where a young woman is drying tumblers. I don't mean to stop dead in my tracks, but my feet feel like they have cement blocks secured at the ankle. This girl is...*holy shit*. Her gray-blond hair has that perfect beachy wave thing going on that you only see in Garnier commercials. She looks to be a little on the short end, which my six-foot-three ass finds absolutely adorable. Her heart-shaped face is angular and her slightly squared chin has the smallest cleft indent, while her lips—*those lips*. If it didn't look like I had at least a decade on her, I could easily entertain the idea of walking straight up to this mystery girl and slamming my mouth down onto her deep pink, pouty lips. Covertly, I adjust myself through my jeans as she bites down on her plump bottom lip, concentrating, and I have to suppress the groan about to escape my mouth.

Travis stops talking, noticing I'm no longer following

behind, and turns to see what, or *who* has caught my attention.

"Holy shit. They weren't kidding. She's fucking *hot*—"

My open palm quickly finds the back of his head.

"Ow!"

"Quit gawking, she's gonna think we're nuts. Go grab your damn sacred booth and I'll get us something to drink."

"Word. I'll take a Bud."

"You're twenty, Trav. You're getting a damn Coke."

He grumbles under his breath as I approach the bar, ignoring the whispers as I walk by the pool tables. Wiping my suddenly clammy hands on the sides of my dark wash jeans, I take a deep breath. It's only when I'm standing in front of her that I realize I don't know what the hell I want to say.

You're ordering a beer, dumbass. Just breathe.

As if she senses me, the mystery woman looks up from her task and flashes a megawatt smile in my direction and I instantly get a semi. *Are you fucking kidding me?*

"Hey, what can I get you? We have a few specials tonight and a new local brew on tap." Even her voice is delicious. Slightly throaty yet sweet; all but dripping with honey.

"I'm Cole." *Crickets.* "And…you…are?" *Again, are you fucking kidding me?*

"Working." She smirks at me.

"Right. Sorry. Hit my head earlier. Pretty sure I'm suffering some sort of brain damage. That sounded like a pickup line or something. I just know you're new to town, so I figured I'd introduce myself." I rub my hand across the top of my head, distracting myself from continuing with this garbage spilling from my tongue. "I'll take a, uh, Corona and a Coke. *Please.*" I attempt to give her my best smile, in hopes that she doesn't think I eat paste in my free time.

Probably too fucking late.

"How do you know I'm new around here?" She cocks her head, placing her hand on her hip. I notice that her nails aren't shaped into claws or blinged out like most females nowadays. I find that oddly attractive; the natural state of her fingernails. "Is there a neon sign flashing above my head or something?" She gifts me a slight grin as she turns around to get my drinks, and my face gets hot. She fills a glass to the brim with Trav's soda and pops the top off my beer, sliding them both across the bar top.

"No, no. Not at all." I wave her off. "I've just lived here my whole life; I would have remembered your face, that's all."

Smooth, not at all creepy.

"I do have a pretty big head. Hard to miss." She laughs despite herself. "That'll be $7.50. Do you want a lime with your Corona?"

"Nah, I don't like a fruit salad with my beer."

She chuckles as I hand my card over. As she takes it from me, I notice her left arm is covered in a full sleeve of ink; the black and gray swirls cover from shoulder to wrist in intricate designs. I don't have time to study what they are since she strolls to the other side of the bar, her full hips swaying. She has a Malibu Barbie meets Wednesday Addams look about her, and I am digging the hell out of it. Her Misfits cutoff tee and short denim shorts add to the appeal, and as she stands on her tiptoes to swipe my card through the system, I notice her black combat boots. Her calf muscles strain as she lowers herself back down, leading my eyes up her smooth legs to her delectable as—

"Is there anything else I can get for you? *Sir?*"

She's facing me with a smirk when I snap back to reality, and I know I've been caught ogling her...assets. When I don't say anything, she chuckles and approaches. Next thing I know, her tanned, tatted, and toned arm is reaching across the bar.

Kennedy

"KENNEDY."

"Thirty-fifth President of the United States, sure. What's with the history lesson?"

I giggle at his terrible humor, but I couldn't bear to see him squirm any longer after my previous dismissal. I'm not sure if he's always this socially awkward, but I sort of like toying with him. He's my mouse on a string.

He takes my outstretched hand and the shock wave sends a pulsation straight to my groin.

What the hell is that about?

"Cole. But pretty much everyone calls me Palmer."

"Cole…you mentioned that before. But *Palmer*? That isn't a name—it's a hybrid drink."

"Actually, it's my last name, and Ice T was already taken… pretty sure he has that shit trademarked or something."

I begin a slow clap as I smirk up at him, breathing out a laugh at yet *another* lame joke.

"Wow. Incredible."

Can he tell I'm joking?

His eyes narrow, probably shocked that I was coming off a little cold five seconds ago and now I'm complimenting him, but I'm nothing if not an enigma—and *maybe* also a smart-ass. Getting a good look at him now, though, he really is cute. Cute and...*older*. I would guess mid-thirties, maybe? His dark brown hair is short on the sides, and an inch or so longer and laid haphazardly along the top. Bits of that hair are threatening to fall onto his forehead and I'm tempted to brush the locks back. But I don't. I rake him in, skimming my gaze down his face, and take notice of his prominent cheekbones and stubborn chin under all that facial scruff, giving him this air of pure, raw masculinity. His eyes, though? They're almost *pretty*. Deep emerald orbs framed by long, thick lashes. Why is it that guys are always blessed with the most killer lashes and never have any use for them? The world is so unfair.

Cole Palmer is giving off the broody, silent-type vibe. His jeans are faded and ragged, and his plain white shirt is covered by a well-worn flannel rolled up at his forearms, exposing two full sleeves of tattoos all the way down to his knuckles. I'm typically good at reading people, but Cole Palmer defies the basic categories I could dump him in. I can't pinpoint it. Pinpoint *him*.

His thick, sculpted brow lifts high, as if questioning me.

He probably noticed you creeping, you idiot.

"I am. I really am incredible. But, could you do me a favor? Could you say that often? And out loud? Make a real show of it, you know?" He points across the room to a high-top table where some guy sporting a buzz cut, about my age, is seated. "Not to mention it would earn me some brownie points with my nephew, Travis, over there." Palmer smirks at me and I combust on the spot.

I stare at him in disbelief and before I know it, a laugh erupts out of me. I cover my mouth with the back of my hand.

Shaking my head, my lips lift into an incredulous smile. "You're a strange one, Cole Palmer."

And you know...I think I like it.

CHAPTER TWO

Kennedy

MY FIRST SHIFT AT BUCKEY'S is well underway and I haven't spilled a drink on anyone or fallen flat on my ass, so I'm hoping that's promising. It's been over an hour since I met tall, dark, and *daddy* over there, and I can't stop myself from staring every so often. I can't believe he's still here, to be perfectly honest. Though he's nursing the same Corona I gave him, which must be piss warm by now. He looks completely uninterested in the conversations going on at his table, yet when we make eye contact, he perks back up.

I like this game we're playing, handsome.

I decide to top off a few glasses of water at surrounding tables, brushing my arm along the back of his chair as I walk past. When I peer over my shoulder to see if he noticed, the look in his eyes is smoldering and I shudder. His mouth twists into the most delicious grin I've ever seen. Good God, he is attractive. He reminds me of a tougher looking version of this model I've seen, tattoos and all—*what is that guy's name?* Mike Chabot. That's it! I hope my new crush isn't married. I didn't even bother checking for a ring, although knowing my luck with guys, I probably should have.

Walking over to the jukebox to change the music to cater to the college crowd slowly piling into the bar, I devise my next plan of action. "Swalla" by Jason Derulo begins to fill the airspace and I shimmy my way back behind the bar to grab what I need. Corona, *minus the lime,* in hand, I head back over to Palmer's table and set the ice-cold drink in front of him. Two more men have joined their table since he arrived.

"So, your uncle here never introduced us." I hold my hand out for Travis to shake, but he only stares. "I'm Kennedy."

"You—you know my uncle?" He gapes.

"Oh, sure! We go way, way back." I drop my hand to my hip. "Yeah, like an hour ago. He didn't tell you?" Turning to Palmer with my hand on my chest, I feign offense. "I'm hurt. I thought I meant something to you?"

Lobbing his head back, Palmer releases the deepest rumble of a laugh I've ever heard and my thighs clench together at the sound. The other men at the table must not hear him laugh often, since each of their heads turn in unison to take notice of the rough sound tumbling from their friend's lips.

"You're gonna give the kid a damn aneurysm. Don't play with him like that," he says, still chuckling.

I laugh back, focusing my attention around the table at the other men seated alongside the two of them.

"Can I get you all anything else to drink? Food maybe? Kitchen is still open."

As I glance around the table, I make a sweep of Palmer's left hand for a wedding band. Pleased to find that finger bare, I breathe out a sigh of relief, yet I'm not quite sure why. It's not like anything would ever happen between us.

The dark-haired man sporting a solid white tee to Travis' right speaks out first. "Name is Dolan, dear. Rick Dolan, and I'll take a Bud."

I nod, making a mental note of his order, and smile at the others, waiting for any other requests.

"Corona for me. Do you have lime, sweetheart?" The next man, a blond around the same age as the other two, holds out his hand for me to take. "I'm Greg Chase. Haven't seen you around. You new?"

"We do, and I am. Originally from Boston. I guess I need to learn how to blend in more with the locals, huh?" I joke along with the two men. "Maybe go by my last name since that seems to be a trend around these parts." I end up locking eyes with Palmer and my stomach practically bottoms out. Looking at him is like staring into the sun—nearly blinding and too hot to handle straight on.

"What might that be? Just so I know what to call you." Palmer's smirk is back.

I answer in short. "Darling."

"That you are, sweets," doles out Chase, who lifts Palmer's beer in cheers, taking a swig. I snicker at his drink swiping tactic and tuck a wayward strand of hair behind my ear. "But he means what's your last name?"

I offer a smile back. "Darling *is* my last name. Kennedy Darling. It's unfortunate, really."

"What makes that unfortunate?" Palmer leans his broad shoulders into the table, a questioning gleam in those beautiful green eyes. I make sure to lean in just as he had and wet my lips.

"I think most people find that I'm really more of a Devil than a Darling." I wait for his eyes to widen a fraction and the smile to spread across his gorgeous features before I rap on the tabletop with my knuckles. "I'll be right back with your drinks, fellas." I make sure not to glance at Palmer again as I saunter off, not wanting to appear too eager. That doesn't stop me from putting a little extra swing in my step, though.

I'm about to make my way back to their table, drinks in hand, when I realize I forgot to grab Chase his lime. I pivot back and lean over the front of the bar, stretching to grab the garnish, when I feel large hands encircle my waist and pull my ass flush to their groin. My imagination gets the best of me and I'm disappointed to see the cobalt eyes I'm all too familiar with when I turn around, and not my new crush.

Spencer Laurent.

He and I dated last semester. Don't let his stunning blue eyes, dirty blond hair, and boy-next-door appearance fool you; he's a rich, arrogant, and controlling little boy sporting Sperry's and Ralph Lauren. His father, Jason Laurent, owns half of this town and the people in it—or so I'm told. I've never actually had the *dis*pleasure of meeting Laurent senior.

Spencer and I met at a house party of one of his friends, and he, in his deluded mind, believes he's owned me ever since. I can't say I didn't reap some of the benefits of being on Spencer Laurent's arm; the spot all other girls want to be, making me the one all the guys want, but being at his beck and call got old, and I ended things before I moved here for the summer. Unluckily, my new location is his hometown. I've tried to stay civil with him since I called things off, as my future in this town depends on staying on his good side. Occasionally, however, he likes to mark his territory on me like a dog pissing on a hydrant. Tonight is shaping out to be one of those times.

"How late are you working tonight, babe? Some buddies are throwing a party and I want you to come." That earns him a large sigh.

"I'm not closing since Jim doesn't have time to show me everything in one day. So probably around ten or so. I'm beat, though, Spence." I wipe a bead of sweat off my forehead with the back of my hand. "I'm calling it a night once my shift is done." I attempt to weave around him as he grabs my elbow, pulling me tight against him.

"If working here is going to affect appearances, maybe you should consider a different arrangement, yeah?"

I jerk my arm out of his grasp and look around to make sure people aren't watching our exchange. Thankfully, everyone seems too engrossed in their own business to care—except a certain Cole Palmer, whose stare is boring into my flesh. His gaze shifts, and if looks could kill, Spencer would be six feet under, riddled by roaches at this point.

"It's just a party, Spence, and may I remind you that we are *broken up*? Being seen together to"—I make exaggerated air quotes above my head— "'keep up appearances' isn't exactly how this whole thing works." I do my best and put on the sternest face I can muster, hoping he finally gets it.

"Fine," he concedes with a pathetic pout, making me internally gag, because, yes, twenty-five-year-old Spencer Laurent pouts like a child when he doesn't get what he wants. But just as quickly as it arrived, said pout morphs into an arrogant grin. "This weekend, though, you're coming out, even if I have to drag you kicking and screaming over my shoulder."

His ice-blue eyes are like daggers and I find myself having to blink from under his stare. He gives me a hard, wet kiss, bowing me back before he retreats, followed by a handful of his friends.

I finally walk the beers over to their destination, wiping

the remnants of his lips off on my arm, only to find Palmer's seat empty. My body instantly deflates.

Great. So much for that distraction the rest of my shift.

CHAPTER THREE

PALMER

IT'S DARK AND THE AIR is starting to cool when I see that gray-blond hair bobbing out the door of Buckey's. The crown of Kennedy's head is illuminated just so, by the streetlamp outside, that she looks as if she's sporting a halo.

So much for that Devil theory, Darling.

I ended up having to leave before I caused a scene at her place of employment on her first day. That's the last thing I need after what happened a few years ago.

That prick Spencer had grabbed her by the arm like she was his property and instantly my blood began to boil. I've never fucking liked that kid, but seeing his hands on her like he owned her made my feelings exponentially more intense. I have a thing with men grabbing women without their consent, and I've watched his pretty boy ass use and discard more than a few girls in this town for years. Although it's always bothered me, it never truly set me off like it did tonight. The second he placed his hand on Kennedy's perfectly tanned arm, I found myself standing, nearly knocking over the stool I'd been seated on. Chase, Travis, and Dolan looked at me like I was crazy for my sudden outburst and I had to leave the building in order to not step in and color that stuck-up fucking face of his in blue and black.

I heard her say she'd be leaving around ten, so I made sure to be here. I had to come back to make sure he wasn't going to be outside, waiting to pounce when she got off her shift. I shake away that thought as quickly as it came, convincing myself it is only for her protection that I'm standing across the street watching like some kind of perverted stalker.

Get a grip on yourself, man. I internally slap myself.

I'm about to leave, noting that he isn't here to berate her, when I see her backside retreating down the side alleyway of the building. It's not as if Beacon Hill is known for its high crime rate, but damn it all, it's dark, it's late, and she's gorgeous—she should know better than to be walking down dark alleys at night alone.

I look both ways before jogging across the street to catch up to her.

"I hope you keep some pepper spray in that mammoth purse you're carrying."

Kennedy whips around, her eyes widening just a fraction until my face comes into the light and she noticeably relaxes.

"Jesus, to use on you? You scared me half to death!" She laughs, grasping her chest as she continues the way she was heading. "I think I'm safe. This town screams a little more country bumpkin than mean streets of Detroit, know what I mean? I'm sure I can manage the two-minute walk to my apartment unscathed." Her flash of a smile over her shoulder has me trailing behind like a lost puppy.

"At least let me walk you then. You know, ease my unease, and all that."

"If it'll help you sleep tonight, feel free."

I smile to myself as I sidle up to her and she points ahead. "I'm only a few blocks down."

We walk in silence for a few beats, but I can see in my periphery that she keeps looking over at me, almost appearing to be holding something back. Then she speaks, her voice dripping with honey.

"You left pretty early tonight. Have a hot date you were running late for or something?"

"Or something," I quip. "Nah, I'm not usually a fan of starting brawls in public, or beating up dudes ten years or so my junior, so I decided to slip out before I did something stupid." This confession gets her attention.

"You? Start a brawl? I'd like to see that." She laughs. "Who's the unlucky victim?"

I let a beat pass.

"Spencer Laurent."

I hold my breath, waiting for what she decides to say next, but Kennedy only stops dead in her tracks at the mention of his name. I turn on my heel and face her.

"You know him well then?" So what if I'm phishing? The question clearly makes her uncomfortable and she tucks a loose strand of her perfect locks behind her ear. Her teeth tug at her bottom lip. Yep, definitely just sent a shockwave to my genitals.

"Uh, yeah. You could say that. He was my boyfriend."

My heart sinks to the soles of my feet and that anger works its way back into my bloodstream. How the hell could this beautiful, witty, eclectic, mystery of a woman have dated that tool bag?

"Your...boyfriend?" I narrow my eyes at her. "As in, you spent time with and actually *dated* that Abercrombie wannabe? Did you lose a bet or something? He's, uh..."

"A dick?" She finishes for me, with a smile that doesn't quite reach her eyes. "Yeah, I'm well aware. It wasn't ideal and I learned that very fast. Cutting ties with him completely is sort of like defusing a bomb. I'm just looking to do it correctly so I can leave in one piece, ya know? He doesn't like to take 'no' for an answer and tends to suddenly develop a hearing problem when I remind him that we aren't together anymore."

I nod in agreement, although I don't think I fully understand. The guy's a dick: just avoid said dick and call it a day. But what do I know? I tend to speak with my fists, not emotions. All I do know is a flood of unexpected protectiveness sweeps over me again and I don't exactly know what to do with that.

You barely know her. Rein in the superhero act.

When I don't say anything further on the matter, Kennedy continues walking. Her boot catches on a crack in the sidewalk and she trips, attempting to keep her balance, but failing miserably. I react not even a second later, my hands gripping onto her upper arms, steadying her against the brick wall behind her. The feel of her bare skin on my palms hits me like a sucker punch, and I let her go quickly as if she burned me to the touch. Still only a breath apart, she lets out an uncomfortable laugh and I wonder if she felt the same burn I did when our bodies touched. Brushing her hair away from her face, she slumps back and huffs out a breath.

"My name is Grace, apparently. Thank you for that. Thankfully just a bruised ego tomorrow instead of a bruised knee."

I'm not sure what comes over me. All I know is I need back that closeness we had a moment ago. Shortening the distance between us so I'm almost pinning her to the wall, my hands move to either side of her against the brick. We aren't actually touching, but her body goes rigid as if we're pressed up against one another. *She does feel it.* At least I know I'm not imagining things. Her sharp intake of breath has me leaning infinitesimally closer. I can feel her hot breath against my lips—it's a mix of spearmint and lime and I'm high on it, that's how close we are.

Then suddenly it occurs to me what I'm doing, how young she is, and that she smells just like my next fucking meal. Alarms begin setting off all the synapses in my head, shouting *bad idea* and *back the hell away while you can.*

All these warnings and I can't stop myself from staring down at her; the smattering of light freckles along the bridge of her nose, her long lashes, and those plump lips.

Big.

Fucking.

Mistake.

Clearing my throat, I step back and extend my hand in front of me as if leading the way.

"Let's get you home."

Kennedy

I'M ALMOST ASHAMED TO ADMIT how giddy it made me that Palmer stuck around to walk me home. I know he's doing it to be a gentleman, the whole *young women shouldn't be out alone past dark* mentality, but in my mind, I could have sworn he was going to kiss me just now.

God, did I want him to kiss me just now.

I clear my throat and point at the end of the sidewalk we're on toward my one-story red-brick apartment building. "I'm just up here."

When Uncle Jim suggested I work for him at the bar this summer, he was able to secure me a month-to-month deal on this place. I plan to finish painting the walls, and Jim is supposed to be coming tomorrow to help me move in my furniture. *Thank God.* Sleeping on an air mattress really isn't giving me those quality Zs. The building's owner *owes him one* and he cashed in on that favor to get me on my feet. The rent is cheap enough that I can pocket most of what I'm making behind the bar. It's also close enough that I can walk to and from work—apparently with a hot guest in tow.

Neither of us says another word until we get to my front door.

"Well, this is me." I rap on the weathered white frame and chuckle uncomfortably. Turning toward Palmer, I find him standing at the bottom of the front steps, hands in his pockets, just staring at me. "Thank you, you know, for walking me here. You didn't have to do that. Although, I do still technically owe you a beer since you ran out of there so fast. Do you wanna come up?" I toss my thumb over my shoulder. "I'm sure I have some Corona in there. Repayment for walking me home."

Don't seem too eager or anything, Kennedy, Jesus.

He rubs at the back of his neck. "I should head home. I have an early day tomorrow."

I let out a breath I didn't know I was holding as he begins slowly backing away, still facing me.

"Thank you, though…for the offer. Maybe I'll see you tomorrow at Buckey's and I'll grab a cold one from ya. Good night, Kennedy."

"Sure thing. Night, Palmer." I unlock my door, slip inside, and shut it behind me quickly. Leaning my back against the cold, hard wood, I only have one question.

Why am I suddenly so disappointed?

CHAPTER FOUR

Kennedy

STANDING IN THE MIDDLE OF my new apartment, I close my eyes briefly and take in the new smells; the fresh layer of paint coating the walls, the newly mowed grass wafting in from the open kitchen window, and the aroma of tea leaves brewing in my mint green Keurig. It might be afternoon, but it's never too late for caffeine.

I let out a sigh. *I'm home.* It's my place, and damn if that doesn't feel good.

The small, ground level one-bedroom, one-bath unit is only a short walk to work, and close enough to town that there is plenty to do. This place might not be much by anyone else's standards, but moving from Boston where you get a postage-stamp-sized apartment for beaucoup bucks, my little sanctuary feels massive.

Oh, and did I mention it's mine?

I slowly spin in a circle, surveying the space as if I haven't already planned exactly where everything will go. I've mentally filled the entire space with real and imagined furniture and odd knick-knacks. The main entrance walks you directly into the open floor plan, starting at the kitchen. The living room takes up almost all of the uncluttered space, with a small bathroom right off the main living area. A short hallway leads to a spacious bedroom with a walk-in closet. The true selling point, aside from the cheap rent, is the exposed brick walls, mixed medium countertops covering the dark cabinetry, and all the large windows. It is my own little blank canvas oasis.

I adore it.

Yesterday, before I worked my first shift at Buckey's, I had scrubbed the place top to bottom and painted a few of the non-brick-covered walls in muted grays. All I have left to do today is arrange my furniture that Jim is bringing by with his truck. He said he was going to try and grab a few extra hands to assist with bringing in the couch, box spring, and other pieces that most definitely were not fitting into my little sedan.

"So glad you're on the first floor," Jim grunts.

Speak of the devil.

He heaves one end of my sectional through the front door, only narrowly missing the breakfast bar. "Just about threw my back out getting this off the truck. I'm getting old, Kenny girl!"

I can't help but chuckle at this since he is barely pushing forty-three. *Real old.*

"Suck it up, old man," a rough, familiar voice chimes in. "Age is just a number."

I choke on my sip of tea as Palmer's large frame fills the entryway after Jim, carrying the other end of the couch. Hold up...are these two...*friends?*

"Although, I didn't know there was so much shit when I agreed to help you move this stuff in here," he grumbles, his large presence making the small space feel so much smaller.

A snort escapes me. *Real lady-like.* "Well, my shit and I appreciate your help if that makes it any better," I say over my shoulder on my walk to the fridge. I grab two of the beers I had ready and bring them over to them as they situate the couch just so. "Here. Repayment by Miss Stella Artois herself."

Taking the drinks from me, both men twist off the caps and tip them back, each swallowing half the contents in a few gulps.

"Thank you, sweetie. Glad to help." Jim croons as I lean up on my toes and peck a kiss onto his cheek in response.

Over his shoulder, I see Palmer watching our exchange as he runs a hand over the top of his head, messing his hair back into the perfect state of disarray in which it always seems to be. I offer a small smile his way in thanks, although I would much rather show him my thanks another way.

Palmer

HOW PATHETIC AM I THAT I get a chubby watching Kennedy stretch up onto her toes to kiss her uncle's cheek? Honestly, being jealous of her uncle is a completely new level of depravity, even for me. My mind just can't help but run rampant, thinking about what those luscious lips would feel like brushing against *my* cheek, suckling along the base of my ear, trailing down my neck and chest. Those plump lips separating ever so slightly as she kneels before me, parting my thighs and wrapping said lips around my engorged coc—

"Cole. Hello?" Jim waves his hands in front of my face, trying to get my attention. "Do you need me to drop you back off at the shop?"

Shit.

I turn my back to him to peer out the window, at what I'm not sure, but mainly just so Jim can't see me adjusting myself through my jeans after thinking about defiling his niece.

"Yeah." I clear my throat. "Yes, that would be great. Thank you."

We bring a few smaller items into the apartment, and with Kennedy's help this time, it goes much quicker. Before I know it, we're out the door and onto the short drive across town to my shop. Jim's terrible taste in music is slowly drowning out the explicit thoughts of Kennedy. Nothing like some fucking Luke Bryan to kill a boner.

As Jim pulls his beat-up Chevy to the curb, I attempt to hop out, but he stops me, extending a fifty between his index and middle finger.

"No need, man. I'm happy to help out wherever I can. Seriously." I wave off the gesture. Maybe one day the folks in this town won't still think of me as just an asshole with a bad temper. I can only dream, right?

As if reading my thoughts, Jim pats me on the shoulder. "You're a good man, Palmer, no matter what they say about ya."

FIVE OIL CHANGES, A FEW tire rotations, an assload of paperwork done and I'm still thinking about Kennedy in a less than virtuous light. *What is the deal?* She is far too young for me, for one, and even if that was a non-issue, I consider Jim a friend—I could never tarnish his family like that. He's been one of the only people in this damn town who never treated me differently after what I did. That means something to me. I won't let this little obsession with his niece ruin that. I can't.

A knock on my office door snaps me out of my thoughts as Dolan walks in. He swings a set of keys around his index finger with a grin, stopping only to rub his hands together. His smile grows.

"Fixed her up pretty for ya. Wait till you see what color I picked out for your baby." He bounces up and down on the balls of his feet, his eyes lit up like a kid on Christmas morning.

Fuckin' fruitcake.

I laugh to myself with how excited he is to show me his latest project. He might be a goofball, but the dude is a beast with restorative paint jobs, specifically classic cars like my 1968 Chevy Nova. As we walk out back to the private parking lot, I'm suddenly…very confused.

Palming the back of my neck, rolling my head from side to side, I take in the view of my restored beauty. "Didn't you ask me to wait and see what color you picked? It's…black. It was also black before. You color blind or something, bud?"

"Nah, man, it's *Midnight Ebony*," he states with a strange tone. "What do you think? Sexy, right?" He wags his eyebrows at me, and I can't help but grin.

"You do know ebony is just another name for black, right, Dol? It's sleek, though. You outdid yourself with this one." With a clap on his back, I round the exterior, crouching and admiring his fine work. "This is…wow. You did great, man, thank you."

Dolan beams. "Think we've done enough work today?

Let's take her for a spin and cause some trouble. Whaddya say?"

Next thing I know, the key he had been swinging comes soaring toward me. I catch it mid-flight. "Oh, I'm sure we can find some trouble."

CHAPTER FIVE

Kennedy

THE NEXT WEEK AND A half continue with the same routine. I show up to work, mix a few cocktails, pour some beer, make small talk with locals who have no idea who I am, break a few glasses, and sweep up said glasses. I'm starting to get the hang of things being one of the only bartenders on staff right now.

The hardest part is trying to keep a level head during the times when Palmer enters the bar. It's almost as though my body can sense him. I'm so attuned to his every move; my skin prickles on the back of my neck, and goose bumps break out all over my body the second I hear his deep voice conversing with his friends. Even from across the room, he's all I hear. I find myself glancing at him throughout each of his visits, all throughout really, and I know he sees me every time.

Each night I leave Buckey's to find him leaning against the street sign on the corner, waiting at the curb for me. I've come to expect it now, so I'm not sure how I'll feel someday if he's busy or decides to do something more meaningful with his nights.

Why doesn't he do something more meaningful with his nights?

Tonight, un-shockingly, I find him in his usual spot and approach him with a shy smile while his look mirrors mine.

"Hi."

"Hey, you." He pushes himself off the post and clears his throat.

We just stand there grinning at each other like two goofy teenagers. Palmer suddenly breaks the spell and holds his hand out in front of him, as if to lead our way down the alley.

We catch each other up on our days—he was busy at the shop and spent most of it in his office doing invoices and paperwork, all of which is foreign to me since thankfully Jim handles all of that at Buckey's. I tell him about the beer loving patrons of this town that I served today, and we laugh about me only breaking one glass in the last two days. He calls that progress.

When we reach my front door, I turn toward him, truly not wanting to say good night just yet.

"It's been over a week of this and you haven't skinned me alive or shown any signs of collecting ears from victims or anything. I feel pretty confident that if you came inside with me, not only could I finally get you that beer I owe you, but I would live to see another day. How about it?" I put on my best full-fledged smile, hoping tonight he'll finally agree. Palmer snickers nervously and scratches at the back of his head.

"You're killing me. One drink. *One.*" He emphasizes this with his pointer finger in the air and I beam, my heart rate picking up speed, and I let us in my front door.

With a simple flick of the light switch, suddenly this is much more real. Cole Palmer…mega hot, older Cole Palmer is in my apartment.

With me.

Alone.

Holy shit.

Finally having him inside with me, without my uncle as a buffer, I'm much more attuned to my space and how it must look to him, through his eyes. My apartment is very much a reflection of who I am. The varying shades of gray walls mixed in with splashes of black make the small space seem much smaller, but I've grown pretty accustomed to having most everything I own on the darker end of the spectrum. I have my succulents scattered throughout and covering most surfaces; the only plants I can keep alive. My books litter every flat surface. LED twinkle lights wrap around almost everything that can be wrapped around. The dark furniture and a curtain of crystal beads covering the entryway to my bedroom finish off the space.

"Mi casa." I do my best Vanna White impression around the six-hundred-square-foot space. "It's a little dark and dank, but I love it. A little different from the last time you were here, huh?"

Palmer scans the room and is silent a bit too long for my liking.

Probably about to hightail it out of here, genius. He's a grown man and your living space looks like a damn dorm room.

"I like it. It's very…you."

"It's *me*? You can tell that by scanning the room for thirty seconds?"

He stops his appraisal of the space and our eyes meet, holding each other's attention.

"My first thought of you, that day I met you behind the bar, is that you were a little bit of new age goth meets valley

girl…this is exactly what I would imagine that to look like."
He smirks at his own assessment.

"I'm not sure if that's a compliment." I laugh, walking toward the fridge to grab our beers. Not hearing footsteps behind me, I turn, seeing that he hasn't moved an inch and his eyes still haven't strayed from me.

"Trust me. It's a compliment." His look is smoldering.

Hoping my heated cheeks don't give away how those few words affected me, I open the fridge to retrieve our drinks and let the cool air wash over me.

As I straighten myself back out to pop the tops off our beers, I turn to find the entryway empty.

Palmer's gone.

CHAPTER SIX

"ALL I'M SAYING IS I like to know what's underneath the hood before I purchase the car, you know what I mean?"

"Yeah...definitely." *No, I don't know what you mean.*

I'm listening to my best friend Sterling drone on about her most recent Tinder hookup. Sterling picks up a few nights a week now to help me wait tables. Sterling Baker is also a Beacon Hill native and has made my move here more enjoyable. I met her at orientation and we've essentially been inseparable ever since.

She is a natural born flirt, meaning she gets tipped—and well—when she works. We're total opposites in the looks department; her long, straight, dark hair to my light tresses and she tends to dress a little bubblier than I ever have. Sterling speaks her mind no matter what and is the definition of a bull in a china shop. You either love her or you hate her.

Thankfully, it's all love on this front.

"I just think asking for a dick or tit pic is a little sleazy, that's all. Call me old-fashioned."

Sterling whips around from facing the cash register and

gives me the stink eye of all stink eyes. I hold my hands up in mock surrender.

"But I mean, you do you, girly." I throw her a kilowatt smile to appease her and she turns back around satisfied. For now.

The bell to the front door chimes, but we've been so slow I don't even bother looking up. Sterling sees the customer first, and I hear a low purr of approval coming from where she's standing. I look up to find none other than Mr. Cole Palmer seated, alone, in the farthest booth from where we're standing.

Still ticked off about how last night played out, I make sure to avoid eye contact with him.

"Not it," I sing, pressing my pointer finger to the tip of my nose.

"Why on earth would you avoid him? He is so yummy."

Sterling gnaws on her lip and picks up a menu to drop off at his table.

"I made a fool of myself last night. It's a long story. I'd just rather not have to serve him right now." I go back to washing pints.

"I'd be happy to service him for ya, babe." She winks at me and I can't help but laugh. "But you better spill when I get back. I want details!" She slaps my ass playfully with the menu, and I squeal as she traipses over to the other side of the room. Trying to occupy myself and not watch this encounter go down, I decide to make sure she fully stocked the register. Not even a minute later, Sterling is back at my side with her bottom lip jutting out.

"He specifically asked if you could take his order. Sorry, babe, I tried." She shrugs.

Shit.

Finally braving a look across the room, I find his green eyes burning holes into my flesh, looking annoyingly gorgeous and broody.

With a sigh, I exit the bar and head for his booth, making sure my face matches his cool demeanor.

"What do you want?"

"Is that how you greet all your customers or am I just special?" He tries for a boyish grin, but I won't let myself react to it.

"It is when said customer bails without a word and then personally requests me to take their order. So, again I ask, what do you want?" It's hard being this cold and detached when his face is so beautiful to look at. I have to brace my hand on the table to keep my traitorous legs from trembling beneath me. I watch his chiseled jaw work under his skin as he plans his next words carefully.

"I want to apologize. I didn't intend to leave without saying anything. I realize I'm the one who initiated our walks to your place and then you were kind enough to offer me a drink and I was an asshole in return. I'm sorry."

His hand covers mine on the tabletop, and then as if thinking better of it, he quickly removes it. I miss the warmth of his hand on mine immediately, but the sincerity on his face warms the cold air around us slightly.

"Well, I do appreciate you coming down to apologize." I curl the right side of my mouth upward slightly, a hesitant grin. I'm met with the most blinding set of pearly whites I've ever seen, and my knees slightly give out on me. "Ugh, you're forgiven...*I suppose*."

Get a grip. Make him work for it, my God.

"I am hoping that you came here to actually eat, though, as much as I would love to stand here making small talk all day."

"Uh, sure. I'll take whatever you suggest. I really only came to apologize, but while I'm here I might as well eat."

I click my tongue off the roof of my mouth. "I have just the thing."

"Should I be worried?" He cocks an eyebrow.

Walking backward from the table, I put on my most innocent smile. "You'll just have to wait and see."

When I enter the kitchen, I ask the main cook, Misha, to make his signature wings with a side of garlic parmesan potato wedges. My favorite meal we offer. When the wings are ready and piping hot, I set the plate of deliciousness down in front of Palmer and cross my arms over my chest. He looks up at me from below those long lashes until he gets a good whiff of the food.

"Are these…salt and vinegar wings?" He dips the tip of his index finger into the sauce and licks it off tentatively. I clench my thighs together, watching him lick his finger, painfully aware of the current state of my panties. "How did you know salt and vinegar is my favorite flavor?" He eyes me suspiciously.

"I didn't." I shrug. "Let me know if you need anything else."

Instead of waiting for his reply, I head toward the bar. The bell to the front door chimes again, and a six topper gets seated. I check the clock on the wall. It reads 11:02 a.m. And the lunch rush begins.

It isn't until I've taken the order of my next four tables, and easily thirty minutes later that I'm able to fully acknowledge Palmer again. When I look up, he's standing and does a completely adorable little salute before tossing a few bills on the table. I start to make my way over when he mouths something at me.

See you tonight.

My stomach bottoms out and my cheeks burn from holding back the smile threatening to consume my whole face.

Tonight.

CHAPTER SEVEN

Kennedy

LYING BACK, READING A NEW book, some mindless TV playing low in the background, and eating half a box of white cheddar Cheez-It may not sound like much to most people, but I've worked the past twelve days in a row, and I'm basking in my downtime. Pajamas and junk food are the only things on my agenda today.

As if the universe wants to test my sanity, my phone vibrates rapidly, signaling a call. *Uncle Jim.*

Ugh, not today, boss man.

The device nearly topples onto the floor. I whip my arm out to catch it before it falls to an early demise on the hardwood of my living room. With a huff, I pause the episode of *The Walking Dead* I have on as background noise and pick up the call.

"I'm sick," I wheeze into the phone, faking a few coughs, really trying to sell it. "I can't come in today. It's probably *super* contagious."

"Anyone ever told you that you're terrible at that, Kenny girl?" Jim chuckles into the receiver. "Besides, I don't need

49

you to work tonight. I was calling to see if you wanted to come over for dinner. I would love for you to meet Melissa. She makes a mean pot roast, I know that's your favorite."

I mean, it's not, but A for effort, Jimbo.

Jim met Melissa last summer while on vacation in Maine and they really hit it off. Enough so that she ended up moving here after a few months of long distance. He proposed after only six months together; but I guess when you know, you know. And I only know this because Uncle Jim tells me every chance he gets.

If only it were that easy.

I've been so busy since I moved here, trying to work as often as I can, that I haven't had a chance to officially meet her.

"Yeah, actually, I would love that." I mean it, too. Jim is the only close family I have, well, have *left*, which means Melissa is soon to be a part of that small familial unit. I'd like to have a relationship with her. "Should I bring anything?" People do that, don't they? Bring dessert or flowers? Quiche? I am so not a productive adult.

No doubt sensing my internal struggle, Jim laughs in my ear. "No, no. Just bring yourself and a hefty appetite, Kenny girl."

As much as I would like to cringe at his favorite nickname for me, I can't bring myself to. It's nice feeling like a part of something—Jim makes me feel loved. It's been a while since I've felt that. "I do hope you get over that sickness, though. I wouldn't want to catch that nasty bug you have."

I belt out a laugh.

Busted.

"Roger that, I'm feeling much better," I lie. "See you soon, Uncle Jim."

PULLING UP OUTSIDE UNCLE JIM'S beige split-level home, I nervously tug down the hem of my dress to hide the scripture inked on my thigh. I never wear dresses since I feel so out of my element in them, but meeting his fiancée for the first time in cutoffs and a black band tee doesn't seem quite right either. I straightened my hair for the occasion, the locks reaching my lower back, and I even applied slightly less eye makeup than my usual smoky-eye look.

Presentable.

The only thing I kept *me*, were my black boots, since I thought they looked cute with the navy blue, orange, and yellow floral print of my dress. I kill the ignition and swing my legs out, adjusting the flowing fabric as I stand.

Jim is waiting at the front door when I look up, smiling and shaking his head as I approach the front steps.

"You didn't have to change your appearance, Kennedy, I barely recognized you in that!" He waves his hand up and down, signaling my outfit. "Melissa will love you just as you are."

He kisses the top of my head as I ascend, and I wrap my arms around his slightly bulging midriff.

"Just trying something new." I smile, but he's not buying it. He knows exactly how uncomfortable I am in this. I guess it was fun to get all dolled up in a different way tonight, but I don't see myself repeating this regularly.

"Come in, come in! Mel's in the kitchen getting everything together."

It smells delicious—the spices and potatoes wafting

through the air wrap me in a homey smell. The pot roast stewing mixes with the fresh linen air freshener plugged into the hallway outlet and I instantly relax. It's comforting. I hear humming coming from the kitchen as Jim and I walk toward the origin of the delicious smells. I stop in the doorway, observing Melissa at work while Jim crosses the space, ending up at her side. Her back is facing me, black curls resting around her shoulders, while her hips sway to the tune she continuously hums. Jim embraces her with one arm, pulling her head toward his and pressing the gentlest kiss to her temple.

She must sense me standing there watching, and she whips around, her lime green apron flowing around her in such a stark contrast to her dark mocha skin glistening under the fluorescent kitchen lighting.

"Kennedy Darling in the flesh!" Melissa wipes her hands on the checkered towel on the kitchen island and makes her way toward me. "It's so lovely finally meeting you in person—the pictures around the house don't do you justice. You are *stunning*, sweet girl." Her hands find their way to my shoulders, her arms fully extended, and she just stares at me, the biggest smile stretched along her face exposing the whitest teeth I have ever seen. I've seen photos of her on Jim's Facebook page—the two of them on vacation in Maine, their check-ins at various restaurants around New England, and the matching profile pictures they have of Jim staring longingly at Melissa while her head is tossed back in pleasant laughter. They really are adorable.

"It's nice to finally meet you too. I've heard so much about you." With her hands still holding me in place, Melissa looks at Jim over her shoulder. His neutral expression morphs to innocence, and he holds his hands up in surrender in front of him.

Chuckling, he simply says, "All good things, hon, I swear it."

A shake of her head and a slight chuckle is all she gives before Melissa turns her attention back to me. Dropping her hands from my shoulders, she leads me into the dining room where the mahogany tabletop is set with all matching placemats, and dinnerware. A glass of lemon water accents each place setting and Melissa tells me to take my pick of seating. Choosing the side with the single place setting, I pull out the heavy chair and take a seat. Melissa rushes back into the kitchen, urging Jim to take a seat while she brings in the food to serve us.

"She's great, isn't she?" He looks at me for approval, and I nod while taking a large sip of my water.

"She is. I'm so happy for you both. When is the wedding again? I'll have to check with my boss and make sure I get the day off. He's a real slave driver, that one." I cross my eyes and stick my tongue out at him like a child, and he cackles.

"Actually," he begins, cracking his knuckles against the table as Melissa carries in a giant crock-pot full of roast. "That's what Mel and I wanted to talk to you about."

Jim looks at Melissa and her smile radiates as she takes a seat across from me. Clearing her throat, she folds her hands in front of her and leans into the table, creating less space between us.

"I wanted to ask you to be a bridesmaid in the wedding. Only if you would be comfortable, of course." Her smile turns meek and she shrugs. "I know we've only just met, but you're like a daughter to Jim, which means you already mean the world to me too. I would love to have you standing up there with the two of us on our special day. It'll just be a small ceremony—a handful of people from town, close friends and family from my side—nothing too crazy!"

I say nothing for a few moments, caught off guard since I wasn't expecting to be a part of any of the festivities. Thinking about it, getting dressed up, celebrating their love, all the dancing, drinking and laughter…I actually get excited.

"I would be honored, but are you sure?" I look between the two of them opposite me at the table. In both of their matching deep brown eyes, sincerity and hopefulness meet my gaze.

"It would make us both so happy, Kenny girl. Things haven't always been the easiest for our family. I think it is high time we get a chance to make some new memories, don't you? Colby would want that."

My throat constricts at the reference to my brother. It's so rare these days that anyone mentions his name. No one in Beacon Hill knows anything about him, and even the thought of talking about him in casual conversation is still too hard for me. For the past year and a half, I've had to cope with being an only child—it's one of the many reasons I moved here from Boston—too many memories hovering over me there like an ominous cloud.

Fighting back the tears threatening to spill and the vice grip on my throat, I simply nod several times.

Please don't cry, please don't cry, please don't cry.

Colby would want us to be happy, I know that much.

Sensing my discomposure, Jim rounds the table and bends at the waist, pulling my body tight to his. He presses his lips gently to the top of my head and we stay like this for a few moments. Out of the corner of my eye, I see Melissa wiping away an errant tear with the edge of her napkin.

"He would be so proud of you, Kennedy. We all are." With a final kiss to my head, Jim heads back to his seat across the table. "Well"—he slaps his palms against the table's edge— "now that that's settled, wait until you try this roast. It'll change your life." His warm eyes meet mine and the corners of my mouth inch up without me even realizing it. I watch him spoon some of the steaming meat, potatoes, and vegetables onto my empty plate. My stomach gurgles.

Colby loved pot roast.

CHAPTER EIGHT

PALMER

THE BELL CHIMES ABOVE MY head as I cross the threshold into Buckey's. It's packed for a Tuesday afternoon, but it is summer time, so I guess five o'clock somewhere can be any time, any day. I scan the crowd, looking to find those bouncy silver tresses I've recently become infatuated with.

Ah, spotted. Hello, gorgeous.

Kennedy is rushing around like a madwoman, seemingly in fifty places at once, taking orders and delivering drinks. Jim really needs to hire more help around here. She works too much.

Or maybe I just want more time with her...

Realizing I've been standing in the same spot gawking since I arrived minutes ago, I decide to seat myself, making my way to an empty table across the room. Weaving in and out of the crowded high-tops, I accidentally bump someone's back. I turn to say sorry, but realize the someone I just elbowed is fucking Spencer. I narrow my eyes and think better of apologizing, deciding to continue on my way.

Just walk away. Be the bigger person. Channel your inner

57

Zen, or Om, or some shit.

Of course, his big ass mouth just has to open.

"Watch where you're walking, dick." He snickers to his group of friends at the table and my hand clenches into a fist automatically. His smug face is scrunched up, baring his teeth in wicked laughter. Kid looks like a damn fool with his turquoise polo on and...*what even is that on his head?*

"Right..."

Nah, fuck being the bigger person.

"I'm not sure how I missed you sitting there in that fuckin'...*cowboy hat*, Spencey boy. Really plays up that whole douchebag persona you have goin' on." Waving my hand in his general direction, I turn my attention toward Kennedy as she drops off a few beers at their table. I give her a cocky smirk that she returns with a playful shake of her head and an eye roll.

"It's a *fedora*, you prick." He says the word like it's something I should fucking know. "Although I'm not sure you're the best person to be doling out fashion advice. Isn't fluorescent orange more your flavor?" His eyebrow rises, punctuating the end of his question, telling me he knows *exactly* what he's doing bringing that shit up with Kennedy within earshot. Spencer purses his lips my direction, a subtle *kiss my ass, you won't do shit in front of her*. I see her questioning look out of the corner of my eye, and before I start rolling heads, I give a terse nod and carry on to the empty seat a few tables over.

I. Am. Fucking. Fuming.

I take my seat as my labored breaths begin coming out in short, choppy pants. Nostrils flaring, blood boiling, and every cell in my body urging me to throw one good blow to Spencer's spoiled ass mug. This is what I get for bantering back and forth like I'm in high school. I let him burrow under my skin.

Goddammit.

Slamming my fist down onto the table, I tuck my chin to my chest and roll my head back and forth between my shoulders, struggling to ease out the tension. I clench and unclench my fists repeatedly to calm my frayed nerves. With my eyes squeezed shut, I'm struggling to keep my cool. My body is rigid, pulled taut like a freshly strung bow ready to fucking snap. When I finally peel my eyes open and pull myself together, I spy Kennedy standing across the high-top table, a curious smile splayed on her face. I focus all of my attention on that succulent mouth of hers, the soft curve of her Cupid's bow and her plump bottom lip. My anger slowly seeps from my extremities and it's as if I can breathe again.

"I don't get the joke. I don't think I've seen you wear orange once," she quips, resting her forearms on the table, leaning in as to make our conversation more private and giving me a matinee showing down the front of her tank top.

Rather gruffly I reply, "Yeah, he's a shit comedian, that one." I lean closer, my body involuntarily pulling into her gravity. I'm hoping she never does find out what he meant by that. "How late you here tonight?"

"I get off at nine." She tucks an errant lock of hair that falls over her eye, back behind her ear, then her eyes widen. "I get off *work*, I mean. Get off work at nine. Not *get off*, get off, you know. God, you know what I mean." Her struggling is adorable, and I blink a few times, waiting for her to catch her bearings. "You could help me out here…put me out of my misery or suggest we do something. Please." She laughs. "*Anything*."

I'm already mid-chuckle as she finishes her rambling.

Could she be any cuter?

"I'll be here at nine. I'll drive you home and we'll make a movie night out of it or something. Maybe even get you off if the mood strikes and we're feeling ambitious." My boldness surprises even me, and I laugh at her expense. Kennedy reaches out to playfully swat at my arm.

She's smiling, though, and my God, the things I would do to continue seeing that sight every day.

CHAPTER NINE

Kennedy

PALMER MADE GOOD ON HIS promise to drive me to my apartment once I got off work. His *anything* suggestion morphed into a fun game of twenty questions, which soon transformed into much more than just twenty.

I learned that Palmer was quite the athlete back in the day. He played varsity football, hockey and even dabbled in mixed martial arts after he graduated from high school. He prefers sweet potato fries over regular, has a low threshold for spicy foods, has never been on a rollercoaster—and never plans to. He is partial to sci-fi thrillers and horror but covertly appreciates a good romantic comedy from time to time—I'm sworn to secrecy on that last one—my life threatened if the information were to ever leak. He's an avid horror story reader, with Stephen King being his favorite. Each tiny morsel of information I acquire about Palmer piques my interest all the more, drawing me in further.

He talks fondly about growing up in Beacon Hill, how nice it was living in such a small town, knowing practically everyone. He got his first tattoo of a four-leaf clover when he was sixteen. His mother found out and almost kicked him out of the house, but he claims she ended up letting him stay when the tattoo got infected, believing that was punishment enough to deter him from getting more. Now he's covered in them. He told me he was quite the troublemaker in school, finishing fights if he wasn't the one to initiate them. I was told all about the scar shaped like a crow on his elbow that he got from a spill off a jungle gym when he was nine. His eyes light up talking about the day Travis was born and dim while explaining the night he found out his parents were getting a divorce. He never got along with his father, but he still took the split as hard as any kid. My mind reels with all this newfound information on everything that makes up Palmer, and I feel as though I understand him more.

We're splayed out on my couch, *I Zombie* playing low in the background. Palmer's reclined, his hands clasped behind his head, and those corded arms flex as his laugh rumbles through the room. His eyes are pinched tight, a look very close to unadulterated pleasure plastered along his sculpted face, and the sight is blinding. My mouth goes dry. How can one man be so utterly beautiful, yet panty dropping, painfully hot at the same time?

"Hold on. So..." His laughter explodes further. "You mean to tell me you got off the bus...*naked*? How did no one see you?"

"Not naked, no...I had mud boots on and my under-wear." I shrug. "Besides, I was in kindergarten! Stranger things have happened, I'm sure. The bus driver didn't even bat an eye! But my mom nearly died when I stepped off the bus that day. She was with a group of other mothers, patiently waiting for their children, and off I come basically buck ass naked in pink frog booties." I sigh at the memory.

Probably the first time in my life realizing that my mother wasn't quite like everyone else's. All the other mothers cooed and guffawed at my stunt. Not Rebecca Darling. Oh no, she gave me the stink eye all the way to our car, and I got the silent treatment the rest of the evening. I had embarrassed her and that was unacceptable.

"That is pure gold, Darling. I'll never let you live that one down." Palmer drags a hand through his dark, almost black tresses, ruffling the strands just so. "Although I do kind of wish I had been there to see that."

His eyes warm, probably picturing my Shirley Temple curls bouncing, descending those bus steps nude, clad in my boots and little backpack.

"I am *so* glad you weren't there to witness that. Telling you about it now is embarrassing enough." I join in on his laughter until my abs burn and tears form in the corners of my eyes. Exhaling dramatically, I sit up straighter, at the exact moment he does the same. Palmer's line of sight is focused solely on my mouth, and I have little to no warning before his hand gently cups my cheek. I stare into his jade eyes, breathing heavily just before his lips descend onto mine. He draws me closer, his tongue sweeping across the seam of my lips, and my body reacts, automatically opening for him. Wanting, needing more.

I'm lost.

Lost in Cole Palmer.

Lost in this moment.

My heart is fluttering, screaming to break free from the confines of my chest, but my head? My head is shrieking at me to pull back.

His thumbs feather across my cheeks as he holds me. His long, tattooed fingers thread their way through my hair, angling my head just the way he wants it, making it easier to devour me, consuming my mouth in an utterly blistering kiss. I moan against him and he makes the sexiest noise from deep within his throat. His hand begins its descent down my neck, and my skin tingles. Palmer trails his hand over my shoulder, and down toward my waist when my phone vibrates on the coffee table, jolting both of us out of the moment.

I hear his quiet groan as I pick up the text.

Melissa: Hi Kennedy! I just wanted to let you know, if you're free tomorrow, a few GFs and I are going shopping for bridesmaids' dresses and I would love for you to come! Let me know, we'll be heading out around 3 pm or you can meet us at the mall if you prefer. Xoxo

PALMER

SHE'S TYPING AWAY ON HER phone, and my heart is practically beating out of my chest.

"Sorry. Wedding stuff," she says. "My uncle's fiancée needs me to go bridesmaid dress shopping tomorrow. I sort of spaced that she asked me to be in the wedding."

I sit up and crack my knuckles. A pillow now rests on my lap, concealing my hard-on from our heavy petting session. Kennedy gets up off the couch and attempts to hide her snicker.

"I should probably head out."

Before I maul you on your couch, pretty thing.

"Okay. Thank you for driving me home."

I chuckle, and pull Kennedy into a quick hug, pressing a chaste kiss to her head. She smells like peaches—my new favorite scent.

"Anytime, pretty lady. Can't have you walking the mean streets of Beacon all alone, now can we?"

I walk back to my car parked out front, adjusting myself in my jeans once I sit down. The motion only succeeds in making me harder, and I silently curse having a dick. Tonight is going to be a long one spent jacking off in the shower to memories of Kennedy's mouth working against mine. Our tongues caressing, teasing, testing, feeling each other out.

I can't fucking wait to do that again.

CHAPTER TEN

PALMER

IT'S ALMOST EIGHT AT NIGHT when I show up at Kennedy's front door, three days after our last encounter at her place.

"Knock, knock," I mutter as I tap the door twice with my steel-toed boot. I faintly hear P.O.D's "Here We Go" in the background of her apartment and smile to myself.

There's some shuffling and seconds later the door whips open, Kennedy's long gray-blond hair flying wildly around her head. I suck in a breath—suddenly feeling like the oxygen has been extracted from around me. She is so fucking stunning. I make an exaggerated show of bowing like an idiot jester at her feet.

"I come with delicious beverages, m'lady."

She giggles and takes the six-pack of beer from my hands.

"I see that, but where are yours?" she teases.

She's barely pushing a buck twenty and we both know she couldn't plow through a six-pack solo to save her life. She does, however, look effortlessly stunning in her black sleep shorts and black tank top. And is it my imagination or is she missing a bra tonight?

God, please give me some fucking strength.

"I thought you could use some brews, and I happen to be glorious company, so, you know...*here I am, and you're welcome.* Besides, I owe you an apology for being AWOL recently. I've been thinking a lot, and I just needed some space to do that." In the past few days, I had been at war with myself.

A part of me wants to steer clear of Kennedy Darling— knowing that she's built for a life much bigger and better than any I could offer her. She should be with someone closer to her age, someone she wouldn't feel uncomfortable being seen with, as a couple.

Or maybe just someone whose past isn't tainted by bad decisions.

The other, albeit much larger part of me, wants to just say fuck it and claim her in front of the whole goddamn world, opinions of others be damned. I'm not quite sure which side won, but I can't stay away any longer. Our kiss the other night has plagued my thoughts ever since, and I need a repeat performance.

Kennedy pops the top on two of the beers and hands one to me, our fingers grazing ever so gently. She gingerly places her forefinger on her bottom lip, playing with the space between her teeth as she heads toward the couch. Making a show of throwing herself down on the love seat with a *whoosh*, she blows the stray blond hairs off her face. Maybe it isn't just me who feels the static pull when our bodies touch like that.

"You're forgiven. *I suppose.* I could definitely use a beer, or five, so thank you for thinking of me." Taking a swig of her Stella, she looks over at me with questioning eyes. "What are you up to tonight? Seems a little unlike you not to be covered from head to toe in grease on a Friday night."

"That's kinda why I'm here. Will you go somewhere with me, Ken? There's somewhere I wanna show you."

Preferably without you running for the hills afterward.

"Sure, just let me change first. What do you have in mind?"

"This something has to be shown, not explained." Holding out my hand, I count the seconds until she grabs on.

I LEAD HER TO THE Nova parked outside and open the passenger side door for her. I very rarely take the girl out of my garage, so instantly I see on Kennedy's face that she thinks something's up.

Elixir, where I'm taking her, is my escape. A buddy of mine is the owner, and I go there every once in a while to blow off steam. In the past, pre-Kennedy, I might pick up a girl, or just drink and watch the shit-show unravel. *Elixir* is the equivalent of The Playboy Mansion, a rock concert and Cirque Du Soleil—on steroids. It's madness and definitely not everyone's scene. It's a hole in the wall warehouse off Broadway and Lafayette Street. My hidden gem within the city outside of town that I've always kept to myself.

Until now.

Her eyes light up. "Cole Palmer being a gentleman and opening doors? Someone alert the media." She giggles.

Even in the dark of night I can see the blindingly perfect smile she gives me over her shoulder before she lowers herself onto the black leather seats. I'd be lying if I said my knees didn't nearly buckle beneath me at the sight.

Fuck. She kills me when she flashes that shit around.

"Just remember you said that in about an hour, Darling." I wink down at her before I shut the door and jog around the front to slide in the driver's seat. I peel away from her side street and head toward the city with my heart in my throat and sweat on my palms.

About thirty minutes later, we arrive at our destination. The sky is muddled with smog from the downtown nightlife, and I pull up to an open spot outside the club. Suddenly my dark jeans and black T-shirt feel stifling.

"Promise me you'll give this a shot," I begin as I angle my body toward the center console, brushing my thumb across her velvet cheek. The contact of our skin against skin shoots off every pleasure sensor on my body like fireworks. "It's a lot to take in, but it's a blast. I just want you to be a part of my other world tonight. Think you can do that for me?"

I sense her apprehension more than she's giving it away—her slight intake of breath, her flushed cheeks and questioning hazel eyes—but to my surprise, she leans forward, pressing those delicious tits together, and stares into my goddamn soul.

Biting her plump bottom lip and making my pants tighter by the second, she simply says, "I trust you."

Kennedy

STANDING BELOW THE NEON SIGN, I read, *Elixir*, in its magenta and turquoise coloring. I've passed this street a handful of times during trips into the city to shop. *How have*

I never noticed this place before? I'll have to drag Sterling out by her hair if this place is as exciting as Palmer is making it out to be. We haven't had a girls' night in so long. I make a mental note to remind her of this fact when I see her this week.

Palmer, clearing his throat in front of me, pulls me from my thoughts and back to this dank and slightly eerie alleyway entrance. Holding his hand back to me, I grab onto it tightly with my left hand and wrap my right hand around his elbow, drawing us closer.

"Let's go. Just stay with me, baby."

Jesus, I'm already wet with his use of those four letters.

We walk hand in hand, with me trailing behind as we head inside the door, bypassing the line congregated outside the entrance. The bass resonates in my chest, "Adrenalize" by In This Moment blaring as we cross the threshold, pushing my heartbeat up into my throat. I'm not sure exactly what I expected, but *wow*. Ignore the fact we just walked past the two bouncers—with a simple head nod as if we were VIP—this place is like nothing I've ever seen before.

Strobe lights and fog fill the space, making it hard to take in everything at once. The first thing I do notice is four stripper poles set up at the front, enclosing what looks like a DJ booth. Each pole has a woman grinding, sliding, and putting on a show for the spectators—fully naked. Their oiled bodies climb up the firehouse looking poles with ease, one flipping upside-down and spreading her legs to show the entire room into her…*well*.

The second woman is spinning around and around, nearly making me dizzy just by watching her routine. The last two women are doing similar acrobatic routines. The lights flashing and the music mixed with the fog make it seem more artistic than striptease, if I'm being honest. I can't tear my eyes away. I hear laughing and a slight tug on my arm has me following Palmer deeper into the massive crowd of people. He makes sure to keep my body tucked close to his.

He says something and I hear him chuckling at my expense, probably noticing my jaw on the floor.

"What?" I yell back over the music. Or maybe it's the intense pounding of my heart. I can't be sure.

Pulling me flush to his chest, he leans down a breath from my ear and yells, "I said, do you like what you're seeing?" Being this close I can distinctly smell his signature scent, something musky, citrusy, and simply masculine. It's a strangely intoxicating and heady mixture.

"Yeah...I'm pretty fond of the view tonight." Locking eyes with him, I try for coy, biting my lower lip, hoping he can pick up my meaning. Tonight, I'm finally going to let on how I feel about him. I just hope he doesn't think I'm crazy for it.

"Fuck, Kennedy, don't look at me like that. I'm trying to keep your virtue here, but you're making it a little hard— *literally*." His hand briefly disappears between us. "Don't test me." He pulls me tighter against him and I can feel his arousal through his tight, dark jeans. I smile up at him like I have no idea what he's talking about and he lets out a groan.

Bingo.

I make a signal with my thumb and pinky toward my mouth that I need something to drink, and he leads the way through sweaty bodies toward the bar. The sleek bar top is made up of dark, almost black wood, and it melts into the atmosphere; as most everything in this place is black. The bartender is dressed like some kind of gothic ringmaster. She's slim, with her average sized chest barely contained within her silver sequined vest. She has a black velvet top hat and short black overcoat. Completely ridiculous, but also completely fitting in this strange and intriguing other world I've just entered.

"Haven't seen you around here in a hot minute, stranger," the bartender purrs. "Who's your little friend?" She looks me up and down.

Little friend? Excuse me, bitc—

Palmer drapes his arm across my shoulders, pulling me to him, and I preen.

"This is Kennedy. Showing her around tonight. It's her first visit."

"Never would have guessed…"

"Play nice, Becks." He scolds. "I'll have my usual, and get this knockout a…"

"Tequila mule, please." I interject, not missing the smirk spreading across his stubbled jaw from out of the corner of my eye.

"What? I know how to party with the best of them." I bump my elbow into his. "Don't underestimate me, Palmer."

I take my drink from the bar top with a smile and slowly insert the thin cocktail straw between my lips and suck a healthy dose to chill my nerves. Not waiting to hear his rebuttal, I shoulder past him to the edge of the dance floor, just to watch. It's only seconds later that I sense him, rather than see him, behind me and it's like static electricity is coursing through my veins. *Just touch me.* I won't be the first one to completely cross that line tonight.

I take in our surroundings; every person here seems dressed to impress and in their own element—leather and chains, sequins and feathers, sweat and liquor—it's everywhere. As I watch the bodies writhing together in a tantric rhythm on the dance floor, I finally feel the heat radiating off him pressing into my back, and his hot breath against my neck. I tilt my head to my right and expose my bare neck to him, taunting him. Palmer skims his lips, barely touching me, from my shoulder to the soft spot just below my ear.

"Dance with me."

It isn't a request.

His husky tone is my undoing, sending a pulsing shock straight to my throbbing core. He doesn't even wait for me to reply before he places his free hand around my hip and walks us, back to chest, into the mass of writhing bodies in the center of the club. "Kill4Me" begins playing, contributing to the heat between my legs.

I turn to face him, draping my arm lazily over his shoulder, as my mule hangs at my side. He tugs me tight to him as we slowly sway together. Being this close, I swear I can feel his heart pounding just as hard as mine. We're sharing the same oxygen, being this close, and I'm drunk on that alone.

"I've never brought a woman here before," he says above me.

This confession makes me uncharacteristically giddy and I bite my lip as I smile to myself.

Hold it together, girl. At least make him work for it a little. This isn't prom night.

"What makes me so different?" I sip my drink. The tart ginger zings my taste buds, warming my body further.

"I haven't quite figured that out yet." He lets out a quiet laugh and my heart literally skips a beat. "But when I do, you'll be the first to know." His stare is intense.

I'm not making it out of this club alive tonight—Palmer will be the death of me.

I down the remaining contents of my drink to give

myself some liquid courage. Just as I finish, Palmer places his other hand at the small of my back, pulling me even tighter against his body, grinding his hardness into my belly, showing me he's right there with me. We grind together, our bodies moving as one. Before I have a chance to react, he darts his tongue out, running up the column of my neck to the spot just below my earlobe, and sucks. *Hard*. My sharp intake of breath has him pulling back to look at me, fire blazing behind his eyes.

"I don't know what you're doing to me, Darling, but I think I like it."

Suddenly, all the warning bells of how this is a bad idea are ringing loud and clear. What if someone were to see us here like this? God, if people found out it would ruin both of our reputations, and then where would I be? I would certainly be a pariah around here if Spencer were to find out about this, making my life hell. I can't afford to leave town and start over again.

I shouldn't be here.

I can't be here.

"Um, sorry. I need to…pee. Can you hold this?"

I hand him my empty copper mug and slink off to the back of the club without waiting for a reply, making my way through the maze of people to get myself to the bathroom. I head down a long, dark hallway leading to the very back of the warehouse. The music sounds farther away as I stumble upon the single stall bathroom where I can finally drop my defenses. Leaning over the sink and staring at myself in the mirror, I take three deep breaths to control my raging libido.

Turns out lady blue balls are definitely a thing. Who knew?

This is why I don't stray from what I know. I play the part, go about my day, no one gets hurt, and things don't get messy. How do I call this off—whatever this may be—without hurting Palmer or pushing him out of my life? I let out a groan as I wash my hands and smooth down a few flyaway hairs. I'm just going to march out there and tell him I feel sick. He'll take me home and I can figure out a game plan from there.

It's fine. This is fine. I can do this.

I shake my head to clear out any negative thoughts and push through the door. Two steps out and I run right into a brick wall. A brick wall with a heartbeat.

Shit.

"Jesus Christ." I laugh uneasily, fearing he can sense it. "You scared me."

"You all good back here? You've been gone a hot minute."

Here's your chance, Kennedy, take it.

"I actually think we should call it a night." I grab my midriff and wince. "I'm not feeling the best. Drank that mule a little too fast, I think." I hope my lie is convincing enough. I can't get into all the reasons this is a terrible idea in the hallway of this sex-infused club.

"You seemed fine just a few minutes ago." His hand darts out to brush an errant hair off my cheek. "Did I scare you off with my dance moves or something?"

He runs the same hand uneasily through his own hair, sending the dark strands every which way, some even falling down onto his glistening forehead.

"No." My voice squeaks, giving me away. "You're fine. Just time to pack it up, I think. I have an early day tomorrow anyway."

"We both have early days tomorrow, Kennedy, we work for a living." He gives me a puzzled look. "What is this about?"

I let out the sigh I've been holding, defeated. Clearly my deception tactics are lacking. "Look…I just can't do…" I wave my finger back and forth between the two of us so he catches my implication. He seems genuinely perplexed by the words coming out of my mouth and cocks his head to the side like a questioning puppy.

"Can't do…*what* exactly? Spend time with me?"

"No, that's not it, I just—"

"Maybe you think you can't do *this*." He mimics my finger wave between us again, cutting me off. "Because fighting the attraction you have for me is easier and safer than dealing with your current miserable situation with Laurent? Am I close?"

My lips part slightly, my breathing turning shallow as he goes on, and lets out a chuckle. Palmer steps forward, forcing me back against the wall. I brace both palms on his chest—to hold myself steady or push him away, I can't quite decide. His large, callused hand brushes the hair away from my neck and he places a hot, open-mouthed kiss in its wake.

Oh. My. God.

Clutching his shirt in my fists gives him the go-ahead to continue and he trails that wet kiss up my neck to nibble on my earlobe. Grabbing my leg behind the knee, he places it over his thigh, pressing his rock-hard body into mine.

"I've wanted you from the moment I saw you, Kennedy." He pants against my neck. "I know I'm too old for you, I know this might be wrong, and God knows I've tried to stay away, but I've been permanently hard for months now—nothing seems to relieve that pressure you're building within me."

If words could make me combust, I would be a blazing inferno at this point. Leaning my head back against the wall, I try to control my erratic breathing. I know I have at least a handful of reasons why I shouldn't be doing this with Palmer. Hell, he listed the main ones just now, but I can't come up with a single excuse good enough to make me not want him while he's pressed up against me. Using his thumb and forefinger under my chin, he tilts my head to meet his smoldering gaze until we're nose to nose. I can feel his labored breathing melding with mine and it's making it harder to resist this.

"I know you want me just as bad. I bet that if I were to peel aside those panties you're wearing, I'd find you soaked for me. Let me show you how it should be—I promise you won't regret it." He searches my eyes for any signs of hesitation. He won't find any. "Let me take you back to your place. I'll strip you out of these clothes and fuck you until even your neighbors know my name."

His cocky little smirk is my kryptonite.

God. Damn.

CHAPTER ELEVEN

PALMER

THE SECOND WE BURST THROUGH her door, we're all lips, tongues and teeth, and I want to do my own version of a touchdown dance. I've wanted Kennedy for so long, it seems surreal to have her in this capacity. Sure, we've been flirting heavily for a few months now and shared a moment the other day, but this? This is so much better than I ever imagined. Her lips are like velvet and the way she nibbles and teases back at mine has me straining so fucking hard against my zipper I need to rub the heel of my hand against my jeans just for some goddamn relief.

I'm surprised I even got us back to her place. I was tempted more than once to pull over and fuck her senseless on the side of the road. Now that we're behind closed doors, I shove her up against her front door with a growl, closing it and the space between us. I mold my body to hers, loving how warm and soft she is. I kiss a hot trail down her neck, thriving off the little moans she lets out as I make my way down her tight body.

"God, baby, you taste so good. My hand just hasn't done

the job for me lately." She lets out a gasp and arches her back, pushing her perfect tits right into my willing hands. "I have a feeling once I sink inside you, you're going to fucking ruin me."

"I'm having a really hard time convincing myself that we shouldn't be doing this when you talk to me like that," she pants against my neck.

You like dirty talk? Oh, I can do dirty, babe.

I don't expect her to take her shirt off so suddenly, but I'll be damned if it's not the sexiest little striptease I've ever seen. Black lace cups her ample breasts, and I can't wait to get my mouth on them. I lick my lips and she whimpers.

My hands are back on her, tearing the strip of material off her chest before I can register whether or not I've actually ripped it. Whoops. At this point, I don't care.

The second her chest is bare, I suck in a breath because, holy hell, she's fucking pierced. The most perfect pair of tits I've ever seen in my life are right before my eyes, and I'm damn sure going to take advantage of that. Her erect nipples accented with silver twin barbells might as well be the nails in my coffin. I drop my head to take the left nub into my mouth as I begin kneading the other vacant mound of flesh with my hand. I suck and pull the metal between my teeth, making her gasps turn to heady moans. Wanting her to come undone in my mouth, I drop to my knees in front of her. Before she can protest, I unbutton her faded jeans while staring up at her, never once breaking our eye contact. The rise and fall of her chest urges me to keep going full speed ahead. I know she wants this just as badly as I do. I can practically smell her arousal from my new position on my knees—where I belong, worshiping her. I slide the skin-tight denim down her legs and she shimmies with me, aiding me in my attempt to get her naked. Once she's down to her matching black lace boy shorts, I can't help but run my nose along the juncture of her panty line, breathing in her scent.

"Let's take this to the bedroom, baby," I mumble into her skin, staring up at her writhing figure. This is me giving her one last opportunity to make a run for it. What I'm not prepared for is her grabbing the back of my head and pulling it toward her still-lace-covered mound.

"Little impatient?" I chuckle.

"Fuck you," she chides, smirking down at me.

"Trust me…that's the plan."

She lets out a breathy laugh, her body shaking above me, and the sound is magical. I can't pinpoint what it is about this girl that has every cell in my body reacting to her, I just know she makes me feel alive for once in my damn life, and I want to keep that feeling bottled up somehow.

I don't have much time to think about this newfound sensation since little miss 'please fuck me' is all but grinding her pussy against my face. I peel the lacy undergarment down her toned legs, her last line of defense against the tongue-lashing I'm about to give her. I pick her leg up and lay it over my shoulder, opening her up to me. It's dark in her apartment, but there's just enough light streaming in from the streetlamp outside the window to let me see what I'm doing. Leaning in, I see that Kennedy is completely bare.

Fuuuucking hell.

"You need directions down there? If you want, I can—"

I cut off her smart-ass remark with one long lick that has her arching her back off the door.

"I think I can manage to navigate on my own. You're gonna pay for being so mouthy, though, you can count on that."

I continue my travels up and down her center, laving

her folds with my wet tongue. She's drenched and tastes exquisite. I continue lapping, slowly at first, and alternating between more pressure and less, flicking her clit with my tongue before making my way back down again. She grinds against my mouth, and I smile to myself, loving how I make her this way; wanton and needy. I latch onto that sweet little bud and give a few sucks, causing her to moan and fist her hand into my hair. The slight tug she has on my strands urges me to pick up speed, and I suck a little harder on her clit. As I bring a finger up to her entrance, teasing her with just the tip, her breathy "oh God, yes," has me nearly coming on the spot.

I'm hard as granite listening to the noises she makes, and I can tell she's getting close. Her greedy little opening contracts around my finger, pulling me into her. All at once, I plunge in and increase the pressure of my lips around her swollen clit. She curses and throws her head back against the door. Watching her from this angle, grinding her pussy into my face and seeing her arched back is a sight to behold. Adding a second finger and massaging the inside of her walls, I watch her eyes clench tight as her moans get louder and I know it'll just take a moment to push her over the edge.

"You taste so fucking good, baby. I can't wait to feel you come on my tongue."

Her whimpering tells me she needs it and I laugh, burying my face between her legs, and speed up my fingers while increasing my suction. A guttural cry escapes her lips as she convulses around my digits. Wave after wave of pleasure hits her and I milk it for all it's worth. As she starts to come down, I slowly pull out my fingers and place a chaste kiss to the top of her mound. I lick my lips clean of her as I stand up, careful to keep her steady after she just came hard against my face.

"I can't—that was—wow. God, Palmer, my legs. I don't think I can move from this spot."

I laugh, seeing her eyes are still closed, and scoop her up into my arms.

"Not even close to finished with you."

I carry her to her bed and place her on the edge, her short legs dangling.

"I thought I was supposed to be screaming your name so the neighbors are on a first name basis? I seem to recall only calling out the Lord's name." Her wolfish grin does me in and I claim her mouth with mine once more.

"I'm only getting started." I pant. "That was just the appetizer."

She laughs and I swear I feel like the king of the world. Just as I'm taking my shirt off, I hear the front door open and we both freeze.

"Kennedy!"

Who in the fuck?

I'm hard as a rock, sporting the world's bluest balls, and someone decides to pop into her apartment uninvited at—I glance at the clock—fucking midnight?

Suddenly it dawns on me, and I know it does to Kennedy too, considering she's white as a sheet and her eyes are the size of dinner plates. Frantically, she turns to me.

"What the fuck are we supposed to do?" She whisper yells. "He'll check in here first!"

Without giving it much thought, I do the first thing that pops into my head: drop down and roll myself under her bed fire safety style.

This should be fucking interesting.

CHAPTER TWELVE

Kennedy

MY HEART IS HAMMERING SO hard in my chest I feel like it's about to burst and splatter all over my new duvet. I am so, *so* screwed. Minutes ago, I was having the most intense orgasm of my life and practically seeing stars and now I feel like I'm about to blow chunks.

What the hell is he even doing here?

"There you are...I've been calling you all night. Where the fuck have you been? Why is your door unlocked?" The anger in Spencer's eyes is unmistakable, and I instinctively take a step back—the back of my knees pressing into the bed causes me to stumble. "And why do you not have clothes on?"

Oh boy.

"Uh, h-hey, sorry, my phone has been acting up the past few days. I've just been here tonight...reading." *At a club.* "You know..." *Attempting to fuck.* "The usual." *So not the usual.* "I was just about to change. What, uh, what are you doing here? It's really late."

Mid-panic I suddenly remember that Palmer can hear our exchange and is currently lying under my bed with a massive hard-on. I grab an oversized shirt from my dresser and throw it on to somewhat even the playing field of the shit storm about to erupt in my bedroom if Spencer finds Palmer here.

Could this possibly get any worse?

"I was trying to figure out why you left me high and dry tonight and were ignoring my calls. I looked like an idiot in front of the guys, not even having the slightest clue what you were up to, but,"—he sighs— "I'm here now. Make it up to me. It's been too long, Kennedy." His slow perusal down my body, stopping at my breasts, makes me cringe as his lip curls into a smirk. I choke back the bile rising in my throat. I can smell the gin on his breath like pine needles.

"H-how am I supposed to do that?" I'm not sure why I'm even entertaining him, but drunk, angry Spencer is not someone you want to piss off. With Palmer under my bed, though, I have slightly more courage to face off against him if need be. He would step in to put a stop to anything bad.

Wouldn't he?

"I can think of a thing or two."

Spencer clears the distance between us and pushes me flat on the bed. I shimmy toward the headboard in a crab-crawl, creating some much-needed space between us. He tugs my ankle toward him to angle my body just below his with my leg cradled between his thighs. I can feel his bulge through his pants and that sick feeling washes over me again.

"It's been a while since I've had you alone, babe. A man has needs, you know, and I'd be lying if I said I didn't miss your tight, little body. Might need a refresher course." He dips his head, and his lips crash down roughly onto mine. I can taste the mix of liquor and something else slightly tangy on his breath.

"Mmm, fuck, bet you're already wet for me, huh? Just seeing me turns you on that much?"

"Spen—"

He silences me with a finger against my lips before he lowers himself, his hot breath brushing against my ears.

"Remember who this pussy still belongs to and who makes you come like a freight train the next time you decide to ignore me." A ring sounds suddenly, and he moves to answer his phone. Saved by the bell.

"Fuck. Gotta bounce. I'm in high demand tonight." Placing a chaste kiss to my lips, he drags himself off me and shoves a hand down the front of his jeans to situate his hard-on.

Gross.

"And you're welcome." He grins wickedly down at me. "If I didn't have somewhere to be, I'd have you showing me your forgiveness graciously with that mouth. You can think of another way to show me tomorrow, though. I'll text you."

Then, just like that, he's gone.

PALMER

LYING UNDERNEATH THE BED KNOWING that she's naked above me and that fucking tool bag has his hands on her makes my blood boil. My fists are clenched so tight that my fingers are numb.

Pathetic. If only everyone who worships him knew that he's a fucking imbecile when it comes to women…

The only thing keeping me underneath this bed and not committing capital murder is the fact that Kennedy and I haven't even talked about what we're doing yet. If Spencer were to catch us in the act, he would make her life here living hell. I can't do that to her, but yet, this forced sexual encounter is just as fucking bad.

I know Kennedy's faking interest—who the hell would believe those moans? An actress she is not, let me tell you. I know how she sounds when she's actually enjoying herself, and trust me, that ain't it. I know, because now that I've had her, I've committed those sounds to memory. A phone rings above me and I hear Spencer's muffled voice, followed by the bed heaving like someone is getting up. Did he really just say *you're welcome* for barging into her apartment unwelcomed and staking his claim like a dog pissing on a hydrant? This guy is unbelievable.

I want to run him over with my truck.

The second I hear the front door close and I know he's gone, I scramble up off the floor. My large frame doesn't cram under beds easily. Duly noted. I look over to see Kennedy sitting upright with her legs crossed underneath her and her head in her hands.

Is she crying?

"Fuck, are you okay? I'm so sorry, that was way too close. I'll go lock the door. I should have before I just…got a little carried away."

When I return, she looks up at me with silent tears streaming down her cheeks and my heart practically shatters. She looks embarrassed and ashamed, and I can't take it. Crawling onto the bed, I reach for her, pulling her onto my lap, cradling her face in my hands.

"I'm gonna figure out a way to get you out from under

his thumb, I promise you. You'll never have to answer to his dumb ass again." I offer a closed lip smile down at her. She nods, a small laugh quietly escaping her lips and the sound makes my smile broaden. I sit, stroking her tears away with my thumbs.

"I'm mortified. I can't believe you had to hear all that. How can you even want to see me again after I had you hiding under my bed like some dirty secret while my asshole ex-boyfriend, who I'm not sure how to fully get rid of, attempts to maul me? It's humiliating and disgusting."

"While I can agree that he was…laughable, you didn't do anything wrong. You're incredible and he will never treat you like his property again in front of me. He can kiss that Sears catalog lookin' face goodbye. I won't hold back a second time."

She nuzzles into my chest and I press my lips to her forehead.

"And look on the bright side," I mutter against her hairline. She tilts her head to look at me, waiting for me to continue. I smirk down at her patient gaze. "At least you got off once tonight."

Her laughter fills the room and I'm on top of the world.

For the second time tonight.

CHAPTER THIRTEEN

Kennedy

IT'S MY FIRST FRIDAY OFF since I started working at the bar, and honestly, I'm not quite sure what to do with myself. I haven't spoken much with Palmer since the other night when Spencer dropped by unannounced. We fell asleep in my bed after he consoled me, my body curved into his as I slept soundly. When I woke, much to my dismay, I found the other side of my bed empty. We didn't even have the opportunity to talk about what the hell happened at the beginning of the night. *Elixir*, coming back to my place and practically mauling each other then…nothing.

Does he regret it? I know he thinks I'm too young, but I hope he knows he didn't force me into anything we did that night. I know *I* don't regret it; I only wish we weren't interrupted and got to see where the night ended up. Though I am tired of his back and forth feelings. One minute he acts like he wants me, and the next he disappears without a word. *Once again.*

My phone vibrates on my coffee table, and I lean forward to snatch it. Hope pools in my belly, just praying for the impossible, that Palmer's name might pop up on my touch screen. Wishful thinking on my part, since we haven't even exchanged phone numbers. Opening the message icon, I see it's from my best friend.

> **Sterling:** Bitch, wanna go to the mall? I need some shoes for my party tomorrow.
> **Me:** Sure, twat. Meet there?
> **Sterling:** I'll swing by to grab you in 10, slut.

Laughing, I decide that boy shorts and a big T-shirt aren't appropriate wardrobe choices for the mall first thing in the morning.

Guess I need to get myself presentable for society.

I settle on some cutoff denim shorts, a distressed, black Palisades T-shirt, and a messy bun. I then toss on some winged liner and mascara, plop my shades on my head, and call my outfit complete.

I hear the honk from outside and I slip on my flip-flops and grab my purse. This is exactly what I needed to clear my head of the other night's monstrosity. Girls' day. Just some retail therapy with my best friend—

Or not.

Descending the stairs, I notice Sterling's red Camry has three passengers in the backseat, one of whom is a certain ex of mine.

You've gotta be fucking kidding me.

"Get in, loser, we're going shopping," Sterling yells out her window, pulling her shades down, and wiggling her shoulders at me, smiling from her driver's seat.

"*Yeah, yeah, Regina.*" My eye roll is only met with a bigger smile on her end. "What's with the kiddos tagging along?" I peer into the back seat as I hop in, to survey the headache that is about to be my day off. Spencer, seated behind Sterling, speaks for her.

"Not shit to do around here, babe. This is Trevor and Keelan. Guys, this is my girl Kennedy Darling. Isn't she a looker?" He winks at me and the three of them exchange words I can't decipher.

"Not your babe or your girl, Spencer. No matter how many times you say it, it doesn't make it true."

"So, that mean you're single?"

I turn my body to look into the rear and take notice of who spoke. The one appointed as Keelan, with dark skin, buzzed hair, and dark eyes meets my gaze first, expecting a response.

"And not looking." I turn my attention forward. "How about we quit the chit chat and get to the mall, ladies and gents?" I up the volume on Sterling's stereo, "Over Now" by Post Malone drowning out whatever they say next, and she peels away from my street toward our destination.

I just hope Spencer takes note of the words.

It turns out shopping with three immature boys is a lot like babysitting.

Too bad I'm not getting paid.

If I have to peel Spencer's hand off my shoulder or my ass one more time, there's going to be a murder scene in the middle of the strip. Sterling got the shoes she was looking for, and I snag a few more band tees, sneakers for the gym, and some ruby red grapefruit froyo. Making our way toward the exit, the boys are hooting and hollering about something, being obnoxious and attracting stares from all over when suddenly my skin begins tingling, almost that static electricity feeling I get when—

"Cole, son! How awesome to see you and your lovely sister. Although I'm shocked, you're not flanked by your two butt buddies." Spencer makes a lewd gesture with his fist and tongue in his cheek.

Palmer motions for his sister to go ahead. She's small in stature, her mousy features hidden behind a short-bobbed haircut. It's odd that in a town this small, I haven't bumped into her yet.

"How long did it take you to come up with that material? Think of it on the spot, did ya?" Cole's uninterested gaze leaves Spencer and drifts to me as his nostrils flare and his gaze turns fierce.

What the hell is he pissed at me for?

"All right, all right…that's enough testosterone for one day." Sterling nods in Spencer's direction. "Palmer, nice seeing you. We were just leaving, weren't we, boys?" She ushers the three of them toward the main doors, tossing a wave over her shoulder.

"You guys go ahead. I'll be right out. I just have to…pee." I stay rooted in place and Sterling shoots me an eyebrow raise that says *sure you do,* as they push through the swinging doors. Spencer gives me one last glance before he leaves the mall, completely out of sight. I turn my attention toward a certain mechanic and cross my arms over my chest.

"You go to school with all those kids?" He nods toward the door they just left through.

"Would you quit calling anyone younger than you *kids*?

You always do that. Most of them are older than me, for crying out loud."

A single brow rises and a smirk appears on his lips at my words. "Would you like to hear what I'd *prefer* to call them instead?"

Rolling my eyes, I walk away. His steps trail after mine.

"Nope." I toss over my shoulder, but he ends up catching up to my side. "And for the record, you don't have any right to be jealous."

His lids fall to half-mast at my words. "Oh, is that right?"

"Yep."

Next thing I know I'm being led by two large hands on my shoulders into the hallway leading to the bathrooms. Palmer's large arms cage me in.

"I may not have a right to be jealous, but it doesn't stop it from being true. I can't just switch that off." His tongue darts out to wet his kissable lips. "It's not like this with anyone else, is it—how we are together?" His gaze lingers on mine, searching for something. "Not to mention, that guy is bad news." He points a finger to the exit door. "And his friends are no different." His palm leaves the wall beside me and finds my cheek. I catch myself leaning in, loving the roughness of his calloused hand against my sensitive skin. "This thing between us doesn't follow the normal rules. You have to know that."

This thing? He can't even call it by what it is. Attraction. Need. *Feelings*. What is he so afraid of? Why is he so hot and cold? I move away from his touch and scoff.

"This *thing* never goes anywhere, because the second it does, you hightail it out and leave me wondering what the hell just happened, Palmer." I sidestep, creating more distance between us. "I'm getting whiplash. You pull me in, call me baby, then disappear without so much as a word. Not anymore. This time *I'm* the one leaving. I'm not a child. If you're embarrassed to be seen with me around town, or think I'm too young for you, then just fucking say so. This whole back and forth thing is eating at me."

I shoulder past him and briskly exit the mall, ignoring him calling my name from where I left him.

When I make my way to the car, I slam the door behind me with a huff.

"Rough pee?" Sterling squints at me, humor evident in her tone.

"Something like that." It's only then that I notice the back seat is empty. "Where'd the three stooges go?"

"Another friend of theirs pulled up. They're heading out to go play pickup basketball or something else equally lame." She grimaces. "But I have a brilliant idea."

"What idea might this be? Better be more brilliant than the time you decided we should get bikini waxes and I got third degree burns on my cooch." I snort at the memory. Never again.

"No, no, no, this is much better than that. I have two words for you." She turns to face me in her seat. "Blind. Date." Sterling holds her phone out, a photo of a young guy on her Instagram feed. He's attractive, with shaggy brown hair, a square jaw, and deep brown eyes. Cute, but definitely not my type—*oh no.*

"Absolutely not. No, I do not need to be set up with some rando. I have enough guy issues in my life already. I don't need to add a new one." I chop my hand through the air in front of my neck, the universal sign for *hell to the no.*

"That's exactly why you need to! Lucas is such a good guy. I've known him for years and he's super interested in you. He saw you at Buckey's a few weeks ago, and he's been asking about you. Plus, I know you have the night off tomorrow, so…"

"I don't know, I feel like that's so weird."

"It's not weird, and he's expecting you tomorrow night for dinner, and then you can both come to my party! It's the perfect plan!" I see the gears turning in her head. Master manipulator, this one.

I let out the groan I've been holding. "You already told him I said yes, didn't you?"

A smile overtakes her face. "Yep. This morning. This is gonna be so fun!"

Yeah…so fun…

CHAPTER FOURTEEN

Kennedy

AS WE WALK INTO THE party at Sterling's parents' house, I'm vehemently glad that there are bodies upon bodies packed in here like sardines. It'll make it easier to slip away unnoticed. As nice as Blind-Date-Lucas is, there's just nothing there—no burning need, no chemistry, and call me crazy, but I've come to need those connections.

I give him a head nod to follow me as I power through the masses in front of us. He spots Sterling before I do, giving her a wave. Relief washes over me. Thank God for my best friend.

You got me into this, so get me out of it. Now.

As we approach, I can smell the booze wafting off her like bad perfume.

"Hey, *lovebirdssssss*," she sings.

"Hittin' the bottle hard, I see." I chuckle at my inebriated friend. Her wet noodle-like limbs end up around my shoulders. Her warm breath tickling my neck as she drunkenly attempts to whisper, "How was it?"

"Where's the bathroom around here?" Lucas' voice cuts

in before I can answer her and I see him scanning the room out of my peripheral. I point down the hallway in front of us.

"Last door on the right." I watch the back of him stroll down the hall away from us and I noticeably relax. Sterling must feel it, and as she pulls back from our embrace, I see her questioning look. I only stare back with an irked expression and a raised brow, clearly not feeling this blind date.

"Nooooo," she wails, dropping her head to my shoulder. "You two are perfect together. Was it really that bad?" she whines, once again meeting my eyes.

"Yes." I nod, grinning at her sad expression over my lack of feelings toward her friend. "He's a nice guy, just not my type, babe. Sorry."

She huffs, blowing her dark bangs off her forehead. "Fine, fine. I guess I need to find him some ass tonight to make up for my failed blind date…setting up…skills." Sterling mysteriously produces two beers and hands me one, hiccupping before traipsing down the hall to find Lucas for round two of matchmaking.

This girl is certifiably insane.

Chuckling, I pop the cap off my bottle using the edge of the countertop and tip it to my lips, enjoying the ice-cold liquid as it glides over my tongue. *So good.* Thankfully, the champagne of beers is washing the red wine taste from dinner out of my mouth. Strike one from the blind date: I hate wine and he ordered for me like I was a child.

I lean against the doorway connecting the kitchen to the living room, bobbing my head to Big Black Delta, content with my people watching. I've always been more comfortable on the sidelines rather than in the thick of the crowd. Spencer was always fighting to bask in the spotlight. At first, he tried to pull me in with him, soon realizing I was much more comfortable standing just to the outside of the center of attention. Back when we were together, even just being with him, that light cast onto me. Everyone knew everything about me, and that's exactly what I left Boston for Beacon Hill to avoid.

I'm alone in my own little world, thinking, swaying to the beat, until something, or rather *someone* draws my attention to the back of the living room. As if I'm dead center of a vortex, all the air seems to draw from my lungs as my eyes meet his emerald orbs. Palmer stands less than a room away, staring directly at me from under hooded eyes.

His look is almost a physical caress. His gaze trails over my exposed skin, causing goose bumps to erupt over my whole body, leaving my flesh tingling. The charge that his perusing eyes leave behind dances across my skin, sizzling, lighting my body on fire.

He is the only person who has the power to elicit this type of reaction from me, the only person I cannot and should not be having these feelings for. I try to pry my eyes away, look anywhere else in the room, but I can't. Not even for a second. I can't *not* look. I'm unable to move from my spot, my feet glued to the hardwood. Unable to think. Unable to do anything but be completely and utterly captivated by Palmer's intense stare.

I haven't seen him since our encounter yesterday at the mall, and he hasn't been into Buckey's for a few days. I only just happened to see him in passing a few days before tonight while picking up some groceries. I saw his scruff covered profile down aisle four and made damn sure to walk the opposite direction. My fondness of him, *okay, maybe obsession*, needs to let up if he's going to continue being so mercurial. I guess it's safe to say I've been avoiding him like the plague.

Not unlike what I'm sure he was doing with me.

Not realizing I have the neck of my Miller High Life in a death grip, I bring the bottle to my lips, still not breaking eye contact until the liquid hits my tongue. I allow myself to close my eyes briefly. I relish those few moments where I can breathe again. When I allow myself to look once more, it's only then that I notice *her*—the woman talking animatedly to him, laughing and squeezing at Palmer's muscled bicep. Her hand glides over his pectorals, caressing him as she continues with her story.

She's touching him.

Touching him like I want to. Like I shouldn't want to.

Touching him as I'll never be able to do in a room full of people we know. This random woman has something with him I'll never be able to have. That he would never allow me to have, since he thinks I'm too young, too immature, too *whatever* the hell his problem is.

Fucking bitch.

Mystery woman turns and stands before him while wrapping her arms around his neck and swaying. To the beat or from too much alcohol, I don't care. All I know is I have to turn away, unable to continue looking at the exchange across the room. I need to leave.

Blindly pushing myself through the mob of bodies, I make my way toward the hallway. My intention is to find Sterling and get the hell out of here, but before I can scope out my friend, I'm jerked by the elbow and pulled into an empty room. Before I can catch my bearings, I hear the soft but slightly threatening sound of the door locking me in and then a soft overhead light switches on.

"Who's the dude?" Palmer's rough growl behind me seems to shake the room around us and I feel him stalk toward me. I might be intimidated if I wasn't so goddamn pissed at him.

Who does he think he is?

"Who's the *dude*?" I whirl around to face him. "Like you have any right to ask that. Who's the *girl*?" I seethe, my face and neck heating up with my unleashed anger.

He thinks for a moment, probably mulling over whether or not to tell me.

"Holly. Went to high school with her. She's the town bicycle and she's drunker than shit. I'm certainly not interested, if that's what you're worried about, since I tend to like my women coherent while I fuck them." He pauses. "Are you going to answer my question? You came here with him." Again, with the telling, not asking. I breathe out a sigh.

Has he been watching me since I arrived?

"He's a friend of Sterling's. Not that it's any of your business, but we were on a date tonight." The happiness I get from saying those words to Palmer's face only lasts a moment.

"You're dating now? I guess I should be glad it's not Spencer, but really?" He scoffs. "That kid looked pre-pubescent, Kennedy." A shadow crosses over his expression. Is it anger? Jealousy? Can't be. He would have to *want* me to actually be jealous, and he makes it clear that he wants nothing public or relationship-like with me. I might be able to call his reaction irritation, but Palmer hardly shows his emotions, so it's tough to be certain.

"You dragged me in here to nitpick at my blind date? Jesus, don't you have anything better to do, Palmer?" The roll of my eyes must set him off, as I watch his slow perusal over my body from the feet up.

"Is that what this outfit was for?" He motions his finger

up and down my torso. "A *blind date*?" he spits out the words like they leave a bad taste in his mouth.

Okay, maybe the multicolored shift dress isn't exactly my usual attire, but since I was attempting something out of my comfort zone tonight, I figured my wardrobe could do the same. The lightweight woven fabric is an artful blush, blue, black, and yellow watercolor print with a rounded neckline and short sleeves. It doesn't show off the girls, but what it covers in my northern region, it severely lacks down below. The hem brushes against my upper thighs, exposing the ink that lies there, and makes damn sure I'm not able to bend forward even the slightest amount without giving the world a show of my bare ass. I paired this with some cute black wedges and I'm wearing my hair in a half pony—the curls cascading down my back in soft waves. In short, I look damn cute tonight and screw him for making me feel less than.

"This outfit is for me, you archaic asshole. I tried something new, and I happen to like it. I'm so sorry that my wardrobe choice offends you, but I didn't wear it for you. Or anyone else for that matter." I'm getting more worked up by the second.

"That's not what—"

"I'm not finished," I cut him off abruptly, my hand held up signaling *stop right there, asshole*. "Last time I checked, I was a grown-ass woman and I can go on dates whenever and with whomever I choose. I do not need permission to do so. And maybe, just fucking maybe, if you hadn't been avoiding me like I was a damn leper the last week, you would know what's going on in my day to day life."

His eyes narrow and his mouth flattens into a hard line as his breathing becomes more erratic.

"Are you done?" He levels me with a heated stare.

"You aren't even going to deny the fact that you've been avoiding me, are you?" I scoff and attempt to exit the door behind him. He stops me with his warm hand on my hip, stalling my departure.

"You're not wrong, okay? Fuck. I have been avoiding you. I had to leave town for a few days just to create some space." He lets out a laugh that rumbles between us. "That's all I did—created distance, physically. You were in my every damn thought and I still craved you. I thought it would help, but it didn't."

He steps closer, his free hand brushing along my jaw, caressing my skin and igniting every nerve ending in my body. "You've consumed my thoughts since the first day I laid eyes on you, Kennedy. You lit a fire within me I've never felt before and it just...it feels right. I know it's wrong, I do. I know I have nothing to offer you that you can't get yourself, and I know that everyone in your life has let you down at one time or another, but you sucked me in and I don't know how to stay away. I've tried."

Looking up at him from under my lashes, I ask the question I've been dying to know the answer to. "Do you actually wanna *be* with me?"

His answer comes in the form of his muscular arms pulling my body flush against his. One hand cradles the back of my head, and the other presses against my lower back, bowing my body to him. My hands brace against his chest and I look into his eyes, seeing his irises twinkling like twin emerald pools.

"I want you however you'll have me. I don't want to share you with anyone—not that wannabe out there, and *abso-fuckin-lutely* not Spencer. I can't offer you fancy cars and a lavish lifestyle like he can, Ken. I live a pretty modest life, but I do well for myself. I never have to debate the extra charge for guac." His light chuckle spreads a smile along my face. "I can afford the gas in my truck, a roof over my head, and I can care for you like no one else can. I've tried to stay away, but I can't. I don't even want to. Not anymore. I don't care what people think of me, what they would think of us, as long as you don't. What do you say?"

He's saying everything I've needed to hear, and part of me feels like I'm dreaming. We stare at each other before what feels like a lifetime passes. I slide my hand up his chest, where it stayed during his speech, to cup his scruffy cheek in my hand. His eyes flutter closed, just briefly, as he leans into my touch. I let my smile take over in that moment and offer him a five-word answer.

"Just fucking kiss me, already."

CHAPTER FIFTEEN

PALMER

I CAN BREATHE AGAIN. I lean in, wrapping my hand around the back of her head, bringing her lips to mine. They're as soft as I remember. Maybe softer. What starts as slow and sensual, quickly turns heated, and Kennedy moans into my mouth.

Are you just gonna ignore the fact that she's still on a date?

I ease up at the thought, pulling back to look her in the eyes.

"What are we gonna do about Mr. Douche out there?" Kennedy tosses out an eye roll and a large sigh.

"Lucas is perfectly nice—"

"*Lucas*"—I scrunch up my face— "is a douche. Point blank, end of story." I press my lips to hers.

"Is that how we're gonna play this? You're gonna pull the jealousy card?"

I nod unapologetically and peck a kiss to her lips once more. "Yes."

"I think he's aware we weren't exactly *jiving*—there's no need to be jealous."

"True. I mean, if anyone should be jealous…it should be you."

She tilts her head, questioning me.

"Holly? I thought you said—"

"No, not her. Mrs. Livingston, you know, the lady at the post office? She was flirting with me hard the other day, trying to get me to help with her *box*." I wiggle my brows for an added effect.

Kennedy laughs and gives me *another* roll of the eyes.

"Please. Mrs. Livingston is pushing eighty and getting help with her 'box' is part of her job description. She asks everyone, you pervert."

"I don't know. She seemed real into it to me."

"You're stupid." She chuckles.

Glad that the tension has completely evaporated from the room, I seize her face between my hands and kiss her once more. Our lips glide across one another and I feel the beginnings of a smile forming as she kisses me back with equal fervor. Suddenly, I'm missing the warmth of her lips on mine. Kennedy drops to her knees before me.

Oh, hell yes, that's what I'm talking about.

"Quid pro quo, right?" One perfectly manicured dark eyebrow arches as she smirks up at me.

"We don't need to do this here. We can wait." I'm silently bashing myself for opening my mouth. "I'm not in any hurry."

I think I'll die if she stands up.

Looking up at me beneath her dark lashes, she mutters, "I am."

Well, hell if I wasn't already rock-hard for this girl…

My jaw tenses as she unbuckles my pants and slides them slowly down my thighs, gliding her nails as she goes. I arch up onto my toes and a growl erupts from my throat. I'm relishing the sting of her nails against my bare legs. She licks her luscious lips as she takes me in hand. My dick looks massive wrapped up in her small fingers.

"Well, damn. Hello there, handsome." She gives my cock a quick kiss at the tip and I swear, I nearly drop to a knee and propose.

The wet heat of her tongue runs up the length of my shaft as she stares up at me, never once breaking eye contact. I fist my hand into her hair, careful to not pull too hard—though I'm sure she'd love that shit, I don't want to press my luck. It's so hard not to do when she parts those lips and takes me into her mouth.

"*Fuck*, Kennedy…"

Her eyes sparkle, even in the dim light of the room we're in. She takes me all the way in, working me into her mouth, her eyes still locked with mine. I break our staring contest first, as I pinch my eyes shut, loving the warm heat of her mouth enveloping me. She takes me all the way to the back of her throat and gulps—the vibration sending chills down my spine.

"Seriously?" I'm panting. I know it. "*Jesus*, don't you have a gag reflex? *Fuck*."

She simply shakes her head as she works me deeper into her mouth. She brings her hands up from their resting place on her knees and begins stroking me in unison with her sucking. Moaning, she picks up her pace. She's a goddamn pro at this. I'm silently reciting the national anthem, thinking of my dead grandmother, that time I failed a spelling bee in front of the whole school—anything to keep from ending this before it's even started. I'm already on the edge as it is.

Kennedy keeps sucking me, bobbing her head and looking at me like I'm the only man in the world. She lets my dick fall from her mouth with a loud *pop*, and she smiles, the sight practically buckling my knees.

"I could do this all day every day." She chuckles.

Me too, baby. Me too.

Taking me back into her mouth, she holds nothing back this time. She works me to the back of her throat and holds me there, pulling me in deeper with her hands on the backs of my thighs. I make some unintelligible sounds as she keeps pumping, pulling the life out of me through my cock. Suddenly, the base of my spine tingles and my muscles are pulled taut.

"I'm about to come, baby...you need to stop unless..."

Ignoring me, she pulls me back into the black hole that is her throat and holds me there, moving her head just so, somehow milking every last drop from my body. I shoot warm rope after rope down her throat and I'm breathing as if I just ran a 5K.

Slowly, she stands to her feet, adjusting her dress and reaching up...*underneath*? Enraptured, I watch her hand disappear for a split second.

Did she really just...? Fuck. She did.

When it comes back out, her glistening index finger is separated from the other four digits, which she presses to my lips. I part them and taste the sweetness off her fingertip.

"That's what you do to me," she says. "Now get your pants back on and let's get out of here—this party sucks."

Have I mentioned I think I'm in love?

I CAN FEEL THE QUESTIONING eyes on us as we try to

race like madmen out of the house, but I don't care. I need to be alone with Kennedy.

The universe has other plans for me and I stop dead in my tracks, practically plowing over her best friend.

Not the kind of plowing I was looking for at the moment, Sterling..

"Uh, hey, guys...I thought I lost you. You've been gone forever, Kenj," she drawls, obviously feeling no pain, and her Cheshire cat grin grows wider by the second. I know she's been waiting for this moment, seeing us out together, since I stepped foot into Buckey's weeks ago asking for Kennedy.

Out of breath, Kennedy stands at my side, her hand still clasped in mine, looking at her friend with a coy smile.

"Hey, yeah, we were just...*talking*. In the other room."

"We were. We were just leaving, though. We have some *things* to attend to. Elsewhere."

I know I'm scrambling, but I can't help it. I have a one-track mind to Kennedy's pussy and I loathe small talk. This is also new to me, as in the last five minutes new, and I'm not sure how to act with her in public. I know I want her, but I don't know how public she's willing to take this right now. The last thing I want to do is push her too quickly.

"What? No! *Stayyyy*. C'mon, Kenny, I feel like you just got here! Please?" Sterling's sad puppy dog eyes don't work on me, but one look at Kennedy and I know she's a goner for her friend.

Annnnd, looks like she's staying. So much for my plans to take her back and finally have my way with her.

Playfully slapping her best friends arm, she laughs, that sound I've grown to love so much. "Fine. But only one more drink. Then I'm out. I mean it, bitch." The two girls giggle and do that weird girly hug thing that they all somehow know how to do from straight out of the womb, and here I am standing around like a lost puppy.

"You ladies have fun. I'll get out of your hair for a bit."

"No!" Kennedy's grip on my hand tightens and she latches onto my forearm with her free hand. "Stay, we'll leave in a while."

We will?

I know I don't have to leave, but this is such uncharted territory with us that I'm not sure how to act. I'm all up in my own head, probably overthinking things already. Why would this stunning girl, this *young* girl want to be cooped up with a bitter asshole like me? Is this just a phase? Why can't I just shut my brain off for ten fucking minutes and enjoy the moment?

"Really, it's fine if you two want to get crazy, do your girly shit. I'm fine leaving early…kinda beat anyway. I can just—"

Kennedy's warm lips meld with my own, silencing me. Everything around me is drowned out. This is no polite peck on the lips. Hell no. This is urgent, feverish. I work my tongue between her lips, as I reach up to cradle her head in my hands. My tongue caresses hers, tasting, feeding, needing her closer than she is. This is a kiss designated for behind closed doors. Private.

Hot as fuck.

Behind us, someone wolf whistles while another one claps, and hooting and hollering ensue. It's only then I remember where we are.

In a living room full of people.

People we know.

People who know *us*.

Guess we're no longer doing this thing in secret.

When I finally, albeit reluctantly pull away, her eyes are sparkling and the beginning of a smile is threatening her lips.

"You are incredible," I say. Déjà vu hitting me from our first interaction.

"No." Her hazel eyes stare up at me, searching mine. "But *we're* going to be."

I place a kiss to the tip of her nose, an unfamiliar calmness washing over me.

"Yeah, I think we are."

CHAPTER SIXTEEN

Kennedy

RIDING AWAY FROM THE PARTY and back to my apartment in Palmer's truck is almost peaceful. His muscular arm is draped over the center console, with his large hand splayed over my thigh. "Bittersweet" by Fuel is playing over the radio as his thumb drums against my leg to the beat. I use this opportunity to study the black ink dancing across his skin, a geometric gear drawing my attention just above his wrist. The intricate black and gray designs cover such an expansive area of Palmer's skin, and I've never really studied the work. They are beautiful. I begin tracing the lines with my index finger, trailing over the gears, flowing seamlessly into the scales of what seems to be some sort of a dragon, moving over to roses sprinkled with thorns. *I wonder what these mean to him.* Not all of my tattoos have meaning; most are just things I love imprinted onto my skin like patchwork, but they are all a part of me, much like these are a part of him. A part I'd love to know more about.

"Wanna grab some food?" he asks, turning down the music.

"I will never turn down food. Ever." He laughs at this and I find myself smiling to the deep timbre sound. Everything about Palmer is so masculine. From his deep and raspy voice to his strong, broad shoulders that lead down to a tapered waist; it's enough to make any female go crazy.

How is he still single?

"What kind of food do you like?"

"I would do unspeakable things for some Mexican right about now." Closing my eyes, I lean my head against the headrest, dreaming of some quality tacos. My stomach rumbles, reminding me I haven't eaten since earlier at the failed blind date, and even that was just a salad. *I'm starving.*

I roll my head in Palmer's direction only to see him staring straight at me. We lock eyes and suddenly I find myself becoming shy, although I'm not sure why. I had his dick in my mouth no more than half an hour ago, and we just kissed in front of an entire room of people, people we know and who will see us again around town. And it wasn't just any kiss...I'm fairly sure we left PG-13 ratings in the rearview during that one. It was wet and passionate and consuming and—

"That sounds delicious," he groans. "I could kill a few tacos...I know just the place."

"WHAT ARE THE MAIN INGREDIENTS you need to make your dream taco?" I hop out of the passenger side and round the truck, meeting Palmer at the main entrance to the restaurant.

"Hmm. Gotta have beef, extra cheese, and lots of salsa. Anything else can be interchangeable. What about yours?"

"Sour cream."

"And?" He looks at me quizzically, his head cocked to the side in pure canine fashion.

"And that's all I *need* in it, I'll put whatever else in… but it's gotta have lots and lots of sour cream." I moan and Palmer laughs, holding the glass door open for me.

"Doesn't take much to please you, does it?" I pass underneath his arm the second he says the words, and we lock eyes. I chuckle, pulling my hair off the back of my neck to secure it all over one shoulder.

"You haven't had a hard time pleasing me so far, so you tell me." My boldness seems to be growing from out of nowhere when it comes to him. A sultry look over my shoulder as I continue walking shows my words must have affected him, as he's still standing in the same spot in the entryway. With a shake of his head, likely to clear the thoughts brought on, he laughs once humorlessly and prowls my direction, placing his hand on the small of my back, and leads us to an empty booth.

"Pleasing you pleases me. Must be why it comes so naturally, and I plan to please you over and over again." His warm breath against my neck erupts my skin in goose bumps as he whispers, "So get used to it, baby."

Hearing Palmer use that specific term of endearment does miraculous things to my insides; it turns me to mush and simultaneously stokes the fire raging within me. Once seated, thankfully, a waitress asks for our food and drink orders, saving me from having to address the current state of my panties due to Palmer's words. Not once taking his eyes from mine, Palmer orders two iced teas: peach for me, sweet for him.

When the waitress finally relieves us, he's the first to break our staring contest, dropping his chin to his chest and lightly chuckling.

"What are you doing to me, Darling?" His eyes slowly rise to meet mine once again.

"Whatever do you mean?" I cradle my chin with my hands and bat my eyelashes.

Before he can answer, his phone vibrates on the tabletop, startling us both. Blowing out a breath and apologizing, he answers the call.

"Yeah?" "No, you cannot take the *girl* for a spin tomorrow." "No, I don't care if you already told her, you aren't driving that fucking car." He laughs and pinches the bridge of his nose. "I will buy you your own shit-box to rebuild from the ground up." "You are such a pain in my ass, kid." His smile grows larger, and he laughs once more. "*Fine.* But one scratch on her and you will be walking with a limp until you're eighty, T, got it?"

Ah. Travis. I should have known.

I laugh, taking a sip of the cold drink placed in front of me as Palmer finishes the call.

"Yeah, yeah. I love you too, kid." Ending the call, Palmer tussles up his hair and takes a sip from his tea.

"You and Travis seem pretty close."

"I wouldn't say we're close, exactly, but we spend a decent amount of time together. I try to be somewhat of a father figure for him since his own father is complete shit."

"That's very noble of you." I smile at him. "I'm sure he appreciates it, and you seemed really happy just now."

"I am happy right now." Our eyes lock intensely, blocking out everything and everyone else. "Happier than I've been in a long time," he adds.

"Is brooding Cole Palmer going soft on me?" I fake a gasp. "No one would believe me if I told them."

"I could toss over a couple tables in here, maybe throw around a few punches to remind people," he says, and I playfully slap at his hand resting atop the table. He uses this opportunity to grasp my hand in his, slowly caressing his fingers along the back of my knuckles.

"There's No Way" by Lauv is playing quietly through the speakers, and I let myself chuckle.

How appropriate for us.

He seems to have the same thought as he brings my hand to his mouth, brushing a soft kiss along each finger.

"Tell me something about you that I don't know. Why did you leave Boston? There's far more to do there than in Beacon Hill. So, why here?"

His line of questioning makes my palms sweaty and I pull my hand from his grasp, placing both of them in my lap. I swallow the lump forming in my throat, mulling over the easiest and most truthful explanation I can give without actually telling him what happened. A little white lie, a slight omission of truth, seems better than the alternative.

"There was a lot of...talk, about me back home. Some stuff went down and instead of dealing with it, I kind of fled. I've made choices I wish I could change and that's why I'm here. I wanted to start over. Make something of myself, I guess."

He nods, a tentative look in his eyes as he seemingly accepts my answer at face value, not pushing for more. I'm beyond thankful for that.

I will tell him. Just not yet.

"Well, you chose a good place to do that. Not much to

do here, but Beacon Hill is a nice place, and I bet it's cool being so close to your uncle now. Does the rest of your family live in Boston? Your parents or any siblings?"

The lump in my throat swells to twice the size and I take a sip of my drink, buying myself some time before I need to give *some* sort of a reply. I'm thinking a measly grunt won't suffice in this situation.

"My dad left town when I was born. I never really knew him. Mom is on boyfriend number five and lives in Illinois now with her newest meal ticket. I think his name is Lars. My mom and I don't see eye to eye on a lot of things. And it's just been me for...a while." I look down at my lap, twirling the edge of my dress around my fingertip.

"Hey." His deep voice softens and I look up to meet his eyes. "I don't want to pry. I'm just curious about this amazing girl who turned my world upside down." He reaches across the table and holds his hand open to take mine, just as our food arrives.

Thank God.

"Now, show me the proper ratio of sour cream to taco... rock my world, Darling." His wink sends my heart fluttering, and I suddenly find myself hungrier than ever before, and not just for food.

CHAPTER SEVENTEEN

Kennedy

IT'S BEEN A STEADILY SLOW day at Buckey's. I would get a table here and there, the occasional small group coming in to get a few beers and play some darts or pool, and a family of six that tipped less than 8 percent.

Today can end any time now.

I'm daydreaming of my couch, Netflix, and all the junk food I can stuff in my face. The last few days have been severely uneventful, and I can't help but blame that on the fact that Palmer has been gone. I received a text message from an unknown number five days ago—I still haven't figured out how he got my phone number—letting me know he was going to be out of town for work; a car convention of some sort. Sure, since he left, we've exchanged a few daily texts, but it's just not the same as being near him, smelling him, laughing with him—

Jesus, Kenj, snap out of it. You sound like a crazy person.

Sure, I do the same routine almost daily, and my life is the same as pre-Palmer, but there is just something missing when he's not around. I can't say that I'm a fan of this new emotion. I know all too well the feeling in my gut while he has been gone; I've experienced enough of it in my lifetime.

Longing.

I'm missing him. I've grown attached without even realizing it. We haven't been, whatever we are, for very long, so it's all still so new, but the feelings I have for Palmer grow exponentially each day.

The front door opening snaps me out of my thoughts. The bell chimes, signaling another customer coming my way. I groan under my breath but make sure to plaster on the best fake smile I can muster.

Until I see *him* and every muscle in my body instantly relaxes, and my smile turns genuine.

"What are you doing here? You're not supposed to be back until tomorrow night." Palmer only smirks.

"You dirty little liar!" My smile spreads; any farther and my face might just split in half.

His shoulders rise and fall. "I couldn't wait. I wanted to surprise you."

"You definitely did. This is an amazing surprise." Then suddenly, reality hits me. "I work for a few more hours, though. I wish I knew."

"That's okay, I'm gonna be sacked out for a while, I'm sure. I'm beat." It's only then that I notice the dark rings under his eyes.

"Do you need anything? Lunch or a drink, maybe?"

Please say a kiss…

"No, I'm good. I just popped in to see you."

My heart squeezes tight at the sentiment. He very easily could have gone home and relaxed until tomorrow night when I was expecting he would be back. Instead, he dragged himself to the bar to see me, even if just for a moment. My insides churn with energy as if I just swallowed half a bag of sour candy.

"Maybe after I'm done—"

"Come over."

"Come over? To…your place?"

"That is what I mean, yes." His signature smirk hasn't left since he walked through the door.

God, I just want to kiss that shit eating grin off his face.

"I'll cook you some dinner."

"You just got home. I can't ask you to cook me dinner," I argue.

"You didn't. I'm offering—or rather *telling*." I know I'm smiling like a fool and I can't seem to stop my facial muscles from contorting.

"Is five thirty okay?"

"I'll take what I can get—five thirty sounds perfect."

Palmer stalks over to the bar where I'm standing, with only a barstool separating us. He leans over the wooden chair, placing his hands on the seat to lean forward. My breathing catches in my throat. The anticipation of his mouth on mine again after so long has my whole body shaking. I feel his hot breath on my lips, just inches away, when the front door chimes.

The trance is broken. Palmer straightens himself, clears his throat, and throws an annoyed look over his shoulder at the older couple who just walked in.

Shit. I almost forgot where we are—can't exactly be making out in front of the customers. Although Jim has claimed he would be okay with the whole *Palmer and me* thing, since he says I'm old enough to make my own decisions and he thinks highly of Palmer, he would be less than impressed to find me sucking face in his bar while I'm on

131

the clock.

Making an effort to look around the bar area to make sure no one is looking, he runs the side of his index finger down my cheek and gives me a wink while backing away slowly.

"I'll text you my address. See you tonight, pretty girl."

AFTER RUNNING BACK TO MY apartment to change into something that doesn't reek of fried food, I decide on an oversized, lightweight black sweater paired with dark jeans and flip flops. I fluff my hair with my fingers and douse it in dry shampoo to give it some volume. Adding another coat of mascara to my heavily smoked out eyes, I decide I'm finally ready to head over to his place. It's been chilly out these past few days, which is a little unheard of in New York mid-June. Even still, I decide to roll the windows down on my drive over, hoping with any luck that the fresh air will calm my nerves.

It only takes about ten minutes to get to his place from my apartment. As I approach the driveway, I take in the layout of Palmer's house. Not what I was expecting from this burly mechanic. His house is a gorgeous slate gray shingled Dutch Colonial. The wraparound porch begins at the front door and continues off to the right side, disappearing around the back. The white accents of the banisters pop against the color of the house, and a beautiful stone chimney stands erect off to the side. This isn't some bachelor pad like the one I was expecting—this is a *home*.

I put myself in park and exit my vehicle on wobbly legs. As I stroll up the front steps to the door, my heart betrays my outward composure that I tried to achieve on the drive over by rat-a-tat-ting against my rib cage. I knock on his front door and hold my breath. With a *whoosh*, it swings open and a barefoot and disheveled looking Palmer stands on the other side of the threshold, shining those pearly whites at me.

"What'cha got cookin', good-lookin'?" I attempt to enter the house, only to walk right into his broad chest—he hadn't moved to let me in.

"Actually…I was thinking maybe we could eat out tonight? I, uh, may or may not have burned dinner." He lets out a nervous chuckle.

I laugh right along with him. "I'm sure we can salvage it. Move it, mister, it's chilly out here."

He reluctantly steps aside for me to enter his home.

The main entryway, colored in muted gray, is very…*organized*. Not a work boot or jacket is out of place on the rack to my right, a rustic Edison bulb chandelier hangs above my head, and the staircase off to the left is painted bright white—in stark contrast to the wall color.

"This is not at all what I was imagining your house to look like," I say almost under my breath as I let myself walk through the rooms leading to the living room.

His amused face tells me he was expecting this admission, "What exactly were you imagining?"

"I don't know." Honestly, I don't. Just not this. This looks like a home built with a family in mind, a wife's touch and attention to detail, lived in with love—something I've never experienced before. "You're just so…*manly*." I laugh. "This house is beautiful. It's just not what I pictured your aesthetic to be." Dragging my hand along the mantle, I take in the framed photos in front of me. One of Palmer with his arm around Travis; a mousy brunette to the side of them. Another of Travis, decked out in football gear, hugging Palmer. Their smiles are genuine, loving. I feel myself smiling as I peruse.

Circling my way back toward him, Palmer extends his hand and I take it. It's large, completely engulfing my entire hand. It's warm and rough in all the right places. "I'll give you the grand tour later." He leads me into his kitchen, and the smell of burnt food invades my senses as we step into the open space. I wave my hand in front of my face to clear some of the smell.

"It's a good thing you're cute." I let go of his hand as I make my way over to the stove to survey the damage. Something charred and seemingly rubber-like lies in the pan. *What even is that?* "Because cooking is clearly not your specialty."

"I was trying to make you some stir-fry since I had all the ingredients lying around, but I got distracted cleaning up and forgot I had something on the stove. The smoke detector works, though, so that's a plus." He laughs as he tosses the carnage into the trash and picks up some takeout menus. "What about pizza?"

"Pepperoni and mushroom?"

"Thank God you're not strictly a 'cheese girl.' I like my women to actually eat."

"Hell no," I giggle. "I need my meat."

Did I really just say that?

The second the words come out, I sneak a peek toward Palmer, and big shocker, his ever-present smirk is plastered across that beautiful face.

"That was actually my plan for later." Hunger flairs in his eyes. I can't speak. All the moisture in my mouth seems to have dried up. Palmer pulls out his cell without breaking our eye contact, only looking down long enough to dial the pizza place. As he orders our food, butterflies begin fluttering in my stomach at the anticipation of his words.

Later.

Later we would be picking up where we left off that night in my apartment. That night with the ending that I've tried since to forget about. The start of that night, though? Burned into my memory. Every touch. Every moan. I can still feel him between my legs, and I ache for him to be back there—moving farther past where we were interrupted. Later, I would finally get to have him the way I've wanted to for so long. His hard length thrusting in and out of me, bringing me to climax, making me moan, raking my nails down his sculpted back, clenching tighter as my orgasm builds while his teeth graze my—

"It'll be about twenty minutes."

Just like that, I'm ripped from my daydream. As if he can sense my thoughts, he chuckles to himself, tossing his phone onto the counter. His hand reaches out once more and I latch on like it's my lifeline as he leads me into his living room.

PALMER

I PLOP DOWN ONTO MY cream sectional, dragging Kennedy's legs across my own. I like her in my space. It feels… natural? Is that what this is?

She lies stretched across my couch, looking even more gorgeous than I remember when I left her five days ago. My hands begin kneading her legs and feet, knowing she's been standing all day working. She rolls her head back on the arm of the couch and lets out the sexiest moan. With no other sounds than the ones her mouth is making, I'll have her naked by the time the damn food gets here.

I need some other noise.

Just then, an idea pops into my head.

"Alexa? Play 'Return of the Mack'." I wait for her reaction as the R&B hit begins flowing through the Echo dot in my living room.

She sits up and her mouth drops open. "How did you know this is my favorite song?"

"I pay attention." I shrug. "Plus, I think it's adorable, this little obsession you have with '90s hits. Especially since you were, what, like four years old when they came out?" I laugh to myself, picturing Kennedy as an angsty teenager, dancing around her bedroom to this shit, her hair bouncing all about. It's a nice image.

A little too nice.

She's still staring at me when I look up, clearly dumbfounded that I might remember this seemingly insignificant fact about her, her favorite song. What she doesn't know is that I remember everything she's ever said or shown to me. I'm like a sponge soaking up all the information that makes up Kennedy Darling, and each new bit of knowledge I gain continuously fascinates me. Has no one ever paid attention to her like this? I find it hard to believe. I mean, she's fucking incredible.

The next thing I know, her leg is swinging across my lap and she's straddling my thighs. Her mouth is on me before I can even process what's happening. Kennedy is frantic, her mouth claiming mine hungrily. She latches onto my lower lip and gives it a tug, which must be attached by string to my dick because up that goes with it.

Goddamn, woman.

She moans into my mouth and I work my arms around her to grab a handful each of her sweet ass, pulling her snug against me. This must be her green light to get some relief as she begins grinding her hips in a figure eight pattern against the bulge challenging my zipper. Her panting breaths are growing louder and more urgent as she kisses her way up my neck, nipping at the sensitive skin below my ear. The continuous friction against my already straining cock is getting to be too much. If she doesn't let up soon, I'm bound to blow my load into my briefs like a horny teenager.

"Baby. *Baby*, you gotta stop," I plead into her shoulder.

Her lips turn up into a smile against my neck, only causing her to buck harder, seemingly racing toward both of our ends. I tug a fistful of her hair, angling her head just so I can whisper into her ear.

"I'm gonna finish if you keep that up, and the next time I do, I *will* be inside you." I gently tug her earlobe between my teeth before pushing her back by the arms, sitting her up straight. Her bottom lip juts out in the most adorable pout I've ever seen. She lets out a huff, her lips puffy and swollen from the assault she was dishing out.

"That was...unexpected," I quip, brushing her hair out of her face and pecking a kiss to her lips. "Unexpected but so damn good." I blow out a breath. "I didn't like not seeing you these past few days."

"Is that your way of saying you missed me?"

Isn't that what I just said?

"Is that lame to say?" I ask.

Her cheeks turn a light shade of pink and she looks down at our laps still pressed together, before looking up at me under dark lashes. "No. It's not lame. If you couldn't tell, I missed you too. More than I care to admit."

I ease her lowered head toward me and press a lingering kiss to her forehead, breathing in her signature peach scent. The doorbell rings and I groan, letting my head fall back onto the couch. Taking this opportunity, Kennedy gently sucks at my Adam's apple, and my blood begins pumping to the nether regions of my body once more.

"Oooohkay, enough of that, you damn tease." I swat her ass and she yips. "Food is here."

I stand with Kennedy still in my arms and turn to place her down on the couch, but instead of releasing her grip on my shoulders, she wraps her legs around my waist, tightening her hold. The bell rings again.

"Looks like you're coming with me. You're a good cover for the tent in my jeans at least. I'm sure the pizza boy isn't interested in the meat I'm packin' anyway." Her airy laughter fills the living room, a sound I haven't heard within these walls for years, as I make my way to the front door.

The teenager delivering our food has eyes as big as saucers when I swing the door open. I watch as his eyes slowly drift down to his front and center view of Kennedy's ass in the air, and he all but drools all over my damn porch. I grunt my disapproval of his wandering eyes. This catches his attention, and I turn to the side, cutting off his direct view as he hands over the pizza box. He has me sign the electronic pad and I add a tip.

Minus two dollars for staring at my girl's delectable ass, punk.

Kennedy giggles in my ear, obviously enjoying this far too much. The teenager wishes us a good night and I thank him, giving her ass one hard smack for good measure before he turns away. Kennedy yelps and I watch as he stifles a laugh while retreating the front steps.

I walk the pizza, with Kennedy still in my arms, over to the kitchen island. The melted cheese, mushrooms, and herbs wafting through my nostrils is a much-needed reprieve from the burnt smell of my failed attempt at dinner. I bend to place Kennedy down on the floor, but still, she refuses to let go. Leaning back, our gazes meet as she traps her lower lip between her teeth. Her next breathy response nearly causes me to go into atrial fibrillation.

"You know, I actually prefer cold pizza..." Releasing her plump lip from the confines of her teeth, she trails her hand down my chest, over my abs, and rubs hard against the front of my jeans.

This fucking girl.

CHAPTER EIGHTEEN

Kennedy

PALMER MAKES HIS WAY UP to his bedroom in record time, with me still tangled haphazardly around his body. We're both laughing as he ascends the stairs two at a time.

Guess we're skipping the house tour and moving straight to the most important room.

He sets me down on both feet once we enter and I'm only briefly afforded a glance around the room before he spins me, shoving me up against the wall. I gasp, feeling his arousal between us.

He holds me there, with his hand pressed against my heart, no doubt feeling the intensity of its hammering beneath my chest. He pauses, just for a moment, raising his eyebrows almost as if he's asking for permission.

I offer him a small nod and his mouth collides with mine. This kiss is frantic, wet, rough and we're swallowing each other's moans, grasping and tugging at each other's clothes. I'm completely lost to his touch. His taste takes over my every thought, until there's nothing left but Palmer. He trails his hand up my back before grabbing a fistful of my hair, yanking my head back, exposing my throat to his rough onslaught. It's all teeth and tongue against my sensitive flesh. My heart continues thundering in my chest, and each beat pounds within my skull in tandem with the throbbing between my legs.

His lips are the most miraculous thing my body has ever come into contact with. I swear it. He licks and sucks his way back up to my mouth and I break the smoldering kiss, just long enough to take his bottom lip between my teeth. I apply just the right amount of pressure to make him groan and grind his hips into mine.

A low growl erupts suddenly from his throat and he pulls me impossibly closer, parting my begging lips with his tongue. His stubbled jaw rubs against my smooth skin and the slight burn has me bucking my hips. I need more.

His hands grasp onto my waist and I'm airborne for only an instant before I land on top of a short dresser. Palmer nestles his body between my parted legs as I pull his shirt up and off, sending the longer bits of hair on top of his head in every direction. Needing contact with his scorching skin, I rake my nails down his sculpted chest and watch in awe at the trailing red marks they leave in their wake.

"*Fuck*…Kennedy." He moans against my neck and when he pulls back, I'm not sure if I imagine his eyes rolling back into his skull or not, but I am loving the power I hold in this moment. I use that domineering momentum and tear my shirt off, leaving me in only my bra and unbuttoned jeans.

Wait, when the hell did that happen?

His mouth is back on me instantly in suckling kisses— my neck, my chest, my shoulder—I moan loudly, unable to contain the need within me any longer. Grabbing a fistful of his hair, I tilt my head, and arch my back just trying to get us closer. I feel his hardness growing between my legs and I grip him through the front of his jeans. He hisses as I apply more pressure.

"Baby…are you sure?" His voice, deep and raspy, is breathless and his chest is heaving.

I close my eyes and lean my forehead against his momentarily, breathing deep, before pulling back slowly and locking eyes with him. "I want you."

He sighs his relief into my mouth as he squeezes me tighter and rubs me through the fabric of my denim pants. The rough friction has me bucking against his hand.

"Can I just tell you that I've been dying to fuck you for the last two months?" He speaks between flicks of his tongue against my lips. "You have no idea how hard it has been trying to keep my feelings platonic."

Laughing, I hop off the dresser and grab Palmer's hand, leading the way toward his bed. I glance back at him over my shoulder. "Can I just tell you I've been silently *begging* you to fuck me for the past two months?" The rumble from within his throat before his large frame topples me down makes me squeal in delight. Pressing me firmly into the mattress, he gives me a quick peck before standing up once more, removing his jeans and boxer briefs. Enraptured, watching this beautiful show before my eyes, I slowly unclasp and toss off my bra. Shivers ripple through me as I watch his devouring eyes peruse my body. He leans down to help peel my jeans and panties off, flinging them in a heap on the floor. Reaching into his bedside table, he retrieves a condom and suits up. I watch, my mouth watering as he rolls it over his impressive length.

Palmer places a knee on the edge of the bed, and I drop my thighs open for him, exposing all of me. I'm not sure where this sudden brazen behavior is coming from, but that's what he does to me. He makes me crazy, my need to be touched completely overshadowing everything else. I'm just a walking bundle of nerves begging to be set off. The length of his hardened rod drags against my sensitive skin and I shiver, closing my eyes. I savor the feeling.

My blood hums in my veins, my need for him threatening to flay me open. He presses just slightly into my entrance. The anticipation is half the fun—he knows it too. I've been waiting my whole life to feel this close to someone, especially someone I truly want, someone I love.

Someone I love.

That's when it hits me like a mac truck: I love him. *I love Cole Palmer.* Not some high school romance, or like any other lover I've had. Palmer is pure fire, burning me inside and out, ruining me for any other man.

And that's just what he is. *A man.*

Any other guy I've been with before fades into the abyss as I'm pinned in place by his intense stare.

Finally, *finally*, he sinks into me, ever so slowly. We moan in unison, and our eyes stay locked on one another.

"Fuck," he groans. "You're so tight, baby. *God.* You feel better than I imagined you would."

When our thighs meet and he's fully seated inside me, I think my eyes disappear into the back of my head. He feels so good, so right. He stills his movements and I open my eyes up to meet his. His green gaze searches mine with hesitancy in his stare.

"You're not gonna break me, Palmer. Hard, fast, rough; I don't care. I just want to still be able to feel you inside me tomorrow."

A devilish grin spreads across his painfully beautiful face.

"You are the perfect girl. How did I find you?" He seals his lips with mine in a quick kiss before slowly pulling out of me. I'm about to protest when he slams back into me. We both groan as the crescendo of our breathing, the slapping of our skin, our moaning and panting fill the room. Palmer keeps a steady rhythm going and the pressure inside me begins to build. He nips at my bare shoulder as I reach around, sinking my nails into his well-built ass, pulling him closer, deeper into me.

Just when I think I can't take the sensations any longer, he slides his large hand between us and begins drawing circles around my clit with his middle finger. My nails rake down his arm and my free hand pulls at his hair. The heady mixture of his steady pounding and tender rubbing finally catch up to me and I feel the tingle beginning at the base of my tailbone. It splinters through me like an electric shock and I explode around him. There are speckled white stars behind my eyelids as the climax tears through me. I scream his name, clawing at his back, my eyes scrunched tight as I ride out my pleasure and come undone beneath him.

"Open your eyes, baby." He coos above me as I pry my eyes open. Palmer's hooded stare makes me feel exposed, which is saying something since I'm bare ass naked in his bed. "I'm about to…*fuck.*"

I graze my nails up his thighs, over the curve of his ass, and through the valley of hard muscles in his back. Palmer bares his teeth and groans, his eyelids fluttering as if he is trying to keep them open to watch me while he comes apart. I will him to groan again. The noises he makes are now my favorite soundtrack of the summer. Finally, his eyes close briefly before opening again, and he pumps one, two, three more times with a groan and spills into the condom.

He slows his thrusts until suddenly, he stops, staying fully secured inside me. Palmer drops his forehead to my chest, panting, and I run my fingers through the top of his hair, damp with sweat. Content and sated, our labored breathing evens out and his body shakes as he chuckles, gently pulling himself out of me.

"That was worth the goddamn wait."

CHAPTER NINETEEN

Kennedy

IT WAS AS NORMAL A Sunday afternoon as any other over the past few weeks and nothing could break the tranquility of our time together. Palmer and I sprawled out on his mattress, the tangled white sheets the only barrier between our naked bodies. I hum my satisfaction against the ball of his shoulder as he traces circles along my back with the rough pad of his thumb. *This is what Heaven must feel like.* That is, of course, until my post-orgasmic fog wears off and my brain begins working again.

"Can I ask you something?" I keep my head tucked between his neck and shoulder as I wait for his response.

"That conversation starter never ends well." He chuckles. "But sure, babe."

"What did Spencer mean that night at Buckey's when he was talking about you in fluorescent orange?"

Palmer's whole body stiffens under me, hopefully just at the mention of Spencer's name. I've seen firsthand how much those two hate each other.

"He seemed to be goading you somehow and I *know*

your uncoordinated ass doesn't hunt." Chuckling, he relaxes slightly. "I guess I just don't get the joke."

"I know I've told you countless times that you're too good to be seen with the likes of me, only you honestly have no idea just how true that is. I've done things I'm not proud of. That little jab he threw at me wasn't just some inside joke." He pauses. "I served time, Kennedy. I spent sixteen months behind bars for beating Jason Laurent within an inch of his life."

The noise my throat makes must have not only been in my head because as soon as I hear the squeak, Palmer's green eyes meet mine in a penetrating stare.

"Not even three hundred feet from the bar where you work daily."

I prop myself up on my elbow and stare down at this beautiful, troubled man. I graze my fingertips along his sculpted chest as my eyes search his, waiting for him to continue. When he says nothing, the one word I need to know escapes from my lips in a breathless whisper.

"Why?"

Palmer's chest rises and falls, me along with it, as he runs his free hand along the top of his head, his tell when he is beyond uncomfortable. As if that one small gesture will keep him grounded somehow.

"A few years ago, Spencer's dad dated my sister, Jaime." He resumes the slow, circular doodles along my back as he stares at the ceiling, telling his story. "What she ever saw in that pretentious dick still evades me, but whatever it was, she was in love with him. Truly. Jason kept her a secret like some pariah, like she was something to be ashamed of. Beneath him, you know?"

I nod for him to continue, though I know he isn't looking

at me.

"The night I got arrested..." Palmer attempts to clear the discomfort from his throat, but it seems lodged in place, so he continues. "I was heading out after a few beers with the guys, and I was walking back toward my truck when I heard a woman struggling down the alley along the backside of Buckey's. I caught a glimpse of Jason under the streetlamp, and I knew, I just fucking knew something was wrong with Jamie. It's like I had tunnel vision after that. I sprinted across the street to get to them, and he had her by the arm, just wailing on her, over and over. *I lost it.* I might have been a scrappy kid in high school, and maybe a little rough around the edges as an adult, but I would never lay my hands on a woman. Never."

"I know you wouldn't." I latch onto him tighter, my heart constricting for this poor man whose heart is beating erratically underneath me. "I know that much about you. You're a good man, Palmer." I press my lips against his tattooed chest, breathing in his woodsy, potent scent.

"I grabbed him by the back of the neck and pulled him off her. I kept hitting him again and again...I couldn't stop. Even after I knocked him unconscious, and my sister screaming at me to stop finally registered in my ears, I just fucking couldn't." His faltering exhale causes my heart to constrict impossibly tighter. Does he actually believe that he was in the wrong? How could he even think that, saving his sister's life like that?

"It took four of Laurent's buddies to pull me off him. I could have killed him, Kennedy. I think I would have if they hadn't gotten to me in time. Sometimes I wish I did." His eyes close briefly as if the memories of that night are strangling him. Leaning over, I press a chaste kiss to his parted lips as his hand cradles the side of my face, deepening our kiss. "I don't deserve you. I almost killed a man, Ken. Granted, he's a world-class bottom feeder, but it doesn't make it right. I hate him with every fiber of my being, but I'm no saint either. My sentence should have been much longer for how bad his injuries were, but I caught a plea deal since my sister testified on my behalf. She told the courts he had been hurting her for some time before that. Fucking bastard didn't even see a moment behind bars for what he did to her."

"I can agree that fighting isn't necessarily the solution to all problems, but I understand why you did what you did. I don't think any less of you—it's just the opposite." His attention that had been on the ceiling for most of his confession turns toward me at my words. "You're a good man, Palmer. You would do anything for your family. You show that every day with how well you watch over Travis, how you protected your sister…you're a *hero*. Seeing that in front of you all those years ago, it's no wonder you weren't in your right mind. Who would be?"

He nods. "Even now, I still only remember pieces of it."

Pulling my arms out from under me, I pull myself up and straddle his hips. Holding my weight off him with my forearm, I use my opposite thumb in effort to smooth out the harsh lines and tension marring his eyebrows, trailing down along each side. I cradle his gorgeous face between my palms.

"Thank you for telling me." I bring my head down to meet where his lies flat on the pillow and kiss him softly.

PALMER

BREAKING THE KISS, I GAZE up into her milk choco-
late eyes, the seductive green rings dancing around their edges
sucking me in deeper. "Thank you for not running for the hills,
or having that same look on your face that the rest of this town
has when they look at me. You've never once looked at me like
they do, not even now." I let out the breath I've been holding
this entire time. Heaviness flows from my chest instantly. The
feeling of finally letting her in is beyond freeing. "Even though
I hate that I put that image of me in your head, 'cause I only
want you to think good things when you see me, I think I
needed that."

"You have no idea how highly I think of you, Palmer."
She pecks my lips, the tip of my nose, and both cheeks in
rapid succession. "You are so good and you don't even know
it, but I'll remind you every chance I get."

If I hadn't already been falling head over heels for this
woman, I would have landed flat on my face in this moment.
I buck my hips up, pressing into her warm body, showing her
just how much that admission means to me, the only way I
really know how.

"Again?" she squeals, throwing her head back and bursting
into her adorable laughter that I love so much. "Aren't you
supposed to tire easily in your old age?"

My palm playfully swats at her round ass and she shrieks.

"Can't seem to get enough of you, babe. You're in my
veins like a drug." And she *is*. I need that subsequent hit of

her, shot intravenously into my bloodstream—my next fix to get me through. I can't imagine not needing her that way. "Now roll over, baby," I rasp and grab ahold of her hip to help flip her off me and onto her stomach.

Pulling herself onto her hands and knees before me, I'm presented with the most delicious view of Kennedy's perfect bare ass, raised high in the air. She wiggles it from side to side like the little tease that she is and my dick stands at attention. The slow burn of desire I have for this woman begins low in my gut and spreads its way outward like splintered glass.

"You say I'm your drug?" Kennedy peers over her shoulder, halting her swaying movements. "So use me."

The invitation falling from her lips is gasoline poured over the fire building inside of me. I fist the base of my cock and waste no time snagging one of the many condoms off the end table. I give myself a few slow pumps as I sheathe my cock. I rub the sensitive head along her slick folds, and her body bucks in response. *That's right, baby*. Slowly, I sink inside her wet heat, and I can fully breathe again.

I'm home.

Owned by her.

I've had her body three times this afternoon already, and still, the hunger remains. It's ravenous. It claws at my insides, like a beast within begging to be let loose. I clench my teeth, attempting to hold in the primal growl I feel working its way up my throat—she just feels too damn good. I continue a steady rhythm, *long slow strokes, tilt up, retreat, slam, long slow strokes, tilt up, retreat, slam*. I know each up thrust is hitting her favorite spot, and not wanting this over in seconds, I draw each slow stroke out longer, forcing her to feel every inch of me.

"Is that all you've got?" She giggles breathlessly, peering back at me once more. "Fuck me already, old man."

Old man? Oh, hell no.

Gathering those silver-blond tresses around my wrist, I roll them into my fist, pulling her head back and exposing her throat. Wrapping my free hand delicately around her jugular, I angle her head toward the ceiling. I up my pace and begin slamming into her, my balls slapping against her sensitive clit with each hard thrust. Each slap melds into the desperate sounds of her panting and my semi-contained grunts. Biting down onto her shoulder just hard enough to leave a slight indentation has her squirming beneath me, her moans turning desperate.

"Be careful what you wish for, baby," I snarl into her shoulder. "I can go ten more rounds. Don't." *Thrust.* "Push." *Thrust.* "Me." *Thrust.*

I apply a little more pressure to her throat, punishing her slit relentlessly as her perfect ass jiggles between us. I feel the spasming between her thighs lasting longer. Knowing she's close, I apply just a bit more pressure to the sides of her throat and tug ever so slightly more on the handful of her waves wrapped around my fist, and she detonates. Kennedy bucks back, meeting me thrust for thrust, calling out my name as the waves of pleasure wash over her. Once her breathing evens out, I press my hand between her shoulder blades, lowering her chest to the mattress with her ass still in the air for the taking. With one hand on her hip, I take my free hand and begin kneading her ass cheek, working my way toward her puckered hole.

"Mmm, yes, Pal—*oh.*"

I gently press the tip of my thumb against her tight ring, halting her words, applying the slightest bit of pressure as I continue my steady assault on her pussy.

"Oh, God *yes*, I'm…*fuck!*" Kennedy's second release milks the last of the restraint I have. The tension that had been slowly building in my spine explodes as I come with her, my release filling the rubber as her name escapes my lips through gritted teeth in a desperate plea. Our breathing finally slows, and I'm crouched over her, still fully seated inside her tightness. I press a prolonged kiss just below her neck and breathe in her scent; peaches and summer.

"Well damn." She lets out a laugh. "Remind me to give you shit in the heat of the moment more often."

I laugh along with her, and the post-orgasmic bliss must have me missing my filter because my next words just tumble out.

"Fuck, I love you."

We both go utterly still. I'm fairly certain I stop breathing altogether. Of course, over the last few months, the thought has crossed my mind. I *do* love this girl. I've never felt more alive than I do when I'm with her. She makes me laugh harder than anyone. Hell, she makes me laugh *period* when I'm normally a grumpy son of a bitch. It's no secret to me that I love her, but I hadn't planned on telling her that tidbit of information just yet.

Pulling out of her slowly and escaping the silence, I leave to discard the condom in the bathroom. I brace myself against the counter, inwardly cursing myself for letting those words slip so casually. What if this is just a summer fling for her? What if she ends up wanting to be with someone her own age? Kennedy is in her prime. She can go anywhere she wants, do anything or anyone she wants. She's twenty-two, for fuck's sake. I scrub my face with both hands and take a leak before strolling back to the bedroom to face the music. I wouldn't be surprised if she bolts. Hell, I wouldn't be surprised if she isn't even in my bed when I return.

Way to fucking go, dipshit.

Kennedy

PALMER PADS HIS WAY TOWARD the bed and I prop myself up on my elbow. The sheet falls, exposing my bare chest to the world, and I watch his gaze drop a fraction, and then his eyes snap back up to meet mine.

"Did you just drop the big L-word and then hightail it out of here like a little bitch, Cole Palmer?" I try but fail miserably to keep the grin off my face. He opens and closes his mouth, floundering like a fish out of water for a few moments before massaging the back of his neck—another of his few telltale signs of discomfort.

He chuckles finally, squatting down on the edge of the bed near me. "Sadly, yes. Not one of my finer moments." He looks terrified, which is not a face I'm familiar with on him.

My hand finds his on the bed and I bring his tatted knuckles to my lips, the softness of them such a harsh contrast to his rough, calloused palms. His apprehensive expression lessens just slightly, most likely calming after realizing I'm still here. No doubt his cynical mind thought I would be long gone.

"Would it ease your mind any if I said, 'I love you too'?" I continue kissing along his knuckles, working my way to his wrist, my eyes never leaving his. "You crazy man." Before

I can say another word on the subject, my face is cradled between those rough hands, his thumbs stroking my cheeks and our lips only a breath apart.

"You couldn't have led with that?" He chuckles. "You have no idea how much better that makes me feel. I thought I scared you off for good." Bowing his head and resting his forehead against mine, he rolls it from side to side. "I haven't been that nervous since…fuck, like high school." His laugh makes my stomach flip.

"You dropped a love bomb in high school? Look at you, Casanova."

"No. Asking Tracey Polanski on a date. She was the hottest cheerleader in the tenth grade. It truly was the peak of my dating history." He smirks and my hand finds his tatted shoulder in a loud slap. He simply chuckles once more, pecking my cheek, my forehead, my nose and then finally my lips. I breathe him in like he's my oxygen.

Breaking our deepening kiss, I give one last peck to his scrumptious lips. "This revelation calls for a little celebration. I vote we order some wings, pop a few beers, and throw on a gory movie. I'll even toss in a super enthusiastic BJ and do that thing you like since I'm feeling so loved tonight." I wink as I scramble off the bed before he can catch me.

Our laughter fills the halls of his empty house and I fling his cell onto the bed for him to make the food order while I freshen up.

After a quick body shower, I toss on one of Palmer's worn, black Metallica tees, sans bra, throw my hair up in a messy bun, and trudge down the stairs to grab our beers.

"What are you feeling movie wise?" I speak into the fridge, searching for the Stella I left here last weekend. "I was leaning more toward gore, but maybe tonight would be a good rom-com night. I know how much you *love* those."

A shirtless Palmer joins me in the kitchen, leaning against the farmhouse sink, his toned and corded arms crossed along that broad, tattooed chest I love so much. My mouth waters at the sight of him.

"Your pick tonight. Especially if I'm getting that enthusiastic head you mentioned earlier. I'm not too concerned with what's playing." He flicks his tongue up and down in my direction and I can't help but laugh. "I like you in my shirts. Let's make that a regular thing."

"Sure, let me just rock out in one of your T-shirts with no pants at work; see how well Jim and the patrons of Beacon like that." I roll my eyes.

"Mmm, right. My eyes only." He fakes a pout. "What a shame."

Who is this ridiculous man and what happened to my brooding mechanic I met months ago?

The doorbell rings, snapping me out of my own head.

That was fast.

Palmer disappears around the corner to pay for our food. I toss the beer caps and deliver the drinks into the living room, plopping myself down onto the couch with a huff as

I tuck my legs up under me. My stomach growls and I rub my belly into submission.

Where are my wings, dude? Wasting away over here.

When a few minutes pass, an uneasy feeling settles in my stomach and I journey my way back into the kitchen to see what is taking so long. Hearing hushed voices at the front door piques my curiosity, and I round the corner to see what the holdup is. To my surprise, as I hang off the doorjamb to inspect the situation, it's not an acne riddled delivery boy I see—it's a woman.

Scratch that, a *beautiful* woman.

She looks very much like a red-headed Heather Graham. Her flowing locks, cut in a long, shaggy bob, frame her heart-shaped face perfectly. Her aquamarine eyes are accentuated by bright red glasses. Dressed in a dark pair of jeans and a flowing beige blouse, she looks petite and so much more put together than I do in my current state of undress. I fold my arms over my chest, remembering how indisposed I am, and lock eyes with her. A sinister smile slowly begins spreading along her perfectly sculpted jawline.

Who in the hell is this bitch?

Palmer, noticing her peering over his shoulder turns, seeing me, his face full of...something. What is that look? Fear?

"*Shit.*" His sun kissed skin pales.

"So, you must be the young girl fucking my husband?"

CHAPTER TWENTY

PALMER

FUCK.

You know when the universe just loves to laugh at you as though you're some minuscule creature? Well, it's funny, I remember as a kid I used to try and fry ants under a magnifying glass, just to watch them burn. Now that's me. I'm the ant.

I guess karma really is a bitch.

No. That's not true. The bitch is Amber showing up at my front door attempting to stir up trouble. Any other time I would just slam the goddamn door in her face, no sweat off my back. But now? Now she's planted a seed in Kennedy's head. Things could not have been going better for us. *Finally.* I told her I loved her, for fuck's sake—and she reciprocated. I've been waiting for what feels like months to say those three words to her, and Amber just shit all over any progress I made.

I can't move. I don't think I've let out a breath since this exchange began a moment ago. *Was it only a moment ago?* Hell, I've probably been standing here looking like a dumbass for an hour for all I know. I should be explaining myself, walking over to Kennedy, wrapping my arms around her perfect, lithe body, and claiming her right here in front of Amber. That'll show that bitch that she doesn't have any bearings on my life anymore.

But I don't.

I don't do anything.

I just stare back at Kennedy's shocked expression. She looks…*shattered*. Standing there barefoot in one of my band T-shirts and little else. She looks absolutely perfect. I can feel her slowly slipping away from me, but I can't form words. She's waiting for me to speak, pleading with her eyes for me to just say something. I open my mouth to speak, to say anything at all, but nothing comes out.

Kennedy slowly nods, a sour look pursing her beautiful features as she backs away, and without saying a word she flees from the room. No doubt about to pack up her shit and hightail it out of my life for good—and still—I stand as motionless and rigid as a statue. Much like the portrait of Medusa inked on Kennedy's unblemished arm, the real-life Medusa on my front porch has turned me to stone. I know I should be running after Kennedy and grabbing her by the arms, not letting her go until she hears me out, but I'm bolted in place. I barely register the words being spoken around me.

"You really should have told her about me, Colson." The sharp arch of her eyebrow mocks me. "Young girls can be really fragile. What were you thinking getting mixed up in that? Can't find someone your own age to toy with, or is that all a part of her allure?"

That's when I snap. "She's twenty-two, not fucking sixteen, Amber. Jesus Christ! She's a goddamn adult and I'm not *toying* with her…*I'm in love with her!*" I can't help my voice from raising. A moment ago I couldn't utter a single syllable and now I can't seem to control the word vomit or my temper. "What the hell are you doing here? You fucked up enough shit in my life last time I saw you, and I made it clear I didn't want that to happen ever again. Now get the fuck off my property before I escort you off by your god-awful hair."

The laugh that escapes her lips is like nails on a chalkboard. It's funny how little things like someone's laughter, that used to bring you comfort, now only makes you nauseous.

"If you think a twenty-two-year-old girl who looks like she does is going to stay with someone nearly fifteen years her senior, you're even more of an idiot than I thought." Amber crosses her arms over her small chest. "She's *experimenting* with you, Colson. That's what girls her age *do*. Did you honestly expect this *thing* between you two to be more than sex? Don't get me wrong, you're good in the sack, but come on. This has daddy issues written all over it. Use your head—not the one in your pants."

The thing about Amber? She knows exactly what to say to cut you to the marrow. Your worst insecurities? She'll find them. Most hurtful words? She'll use them. She touched on every single one of my fears with Kennedy without having ever met her before today. That's just what she does.

I see Kennedy fleeing my front yard out of the corner of my eye and it takes every ounce of strength I have in me not to push this monster out of my way and chase her down. Amber takes notice over her shoulder at the damage she's caused. Her satisfied sneer is present when she faces me once more.

"Get. The fuck. Off. My property." I take a menacing step forward as Amber takes one back. "Now. Don't push me." My words from earlier with Kennedy resound and seize my heart in a vice grip, nearly crumpling me. "Not about this." The last bit practically comes out in a whisper.

Seemingly satisfied that she planted her festering seed, she turns on her heel, hops into her SUV, and backs out of my driveway without looking back.

Kennedy

I CAN'T MAKE OUT WHAT is being said downstairs over the pounding between my ears, but it sounds heated. I have never once, in all the time I've known him, heard Palmer raise his voice.

Until now.

I don't plan to stick around to witness this new side of him either. For all I know, it'll get so heated that they'll be humping like rabbits on his kitchen island in five minutes.

So, you must be the young girl fucking my husband.

Husband.

Cole Palmer. Husband.

Palmer is married? None of this makes sense!

I wipe away the tears that continue to fall, but it's no use. I'm a faucet missing my off knob—the salted streams just keep pouring out. I shove the few belongings I have here into my duffle bag, toss on a pair of jean shorts, and slip on my boots. I can't find my bra anywhere, but I'll have to cut my losses and leave it behind. It's probably in the living room where our clothes started falling off the night before, right before Palmer's mouth latched onto my—

No.

I can't go there. If I do, I'll crumble and I need to get the hell out of here. When I'm back in the confines of my apartment, then I can break down, but not a moment before. I won't give the asshole that.

I slither down the staircase on the opposite side of the house from where the two of them are exchanging words and slip through the back patio. I come around the side of the house, sprinting through the grass to make it to my car parked at the edge of the driveway. I chance a look back toward the front door and see that they're still standing there. At least my humping like rabbit's theory is shot to hell. I shake my relief off—it doesn't matter what he does anymore. He's married. Meaning he's not mine and he never was.

I'm a stupid girl.

I peel out of Palmer's driveway, and this time, I don't make the mistake of looking back.

CHAPTER TWENTY-ONE

PALMER

DAY THREE.

Three days without Kennedy.

Three days without her infectious laughter. Three days without her peach scent filling the airspace between us. Three days without her lingering soft touches.

Three days of fucking hell.

Sure, I've gone longer without seeing her, but not like this. Not with this constant fucking ache in my chest. Not with this crippling sadness that follows me around as I'm forced to trudge through my day to day obligations, all while my heart is fucking shattered. I stopped by Buckey's yesterday to try and talk to her and Jim intercepted me, asking me to give her some space. *Fucking space?* There's already too much space, too much time for someone else to dive in and take her from me when I just fucking got her.

This is what love does to you. It makes you a clingy, blubbering mess. I haven't showered since she left. I don't think I've brushed my teeth. Hell, I don't even think I've *eaten*. Everything feels wrong. I can't sleep, and sleep is all I want as it's the only place I can be with her again, feel her soft skin, touch her gorgeous face and have her scent invade my senses. I merely toss and turn for hours, snag roughly thirty minutes of shuteye, roll myself out of bed with my alarm and trudge through my responsibilities like a damn zombie. I told the guys at the shop I wouldn't be in for a few days. They knew better than to ask any questions.

When Amber left on Sunday, I texted Kennedy. Once the initial shock wore off, I thought better than to follow her. Chasing after her would only close her off to me more. I still had text—I could explain myself. Have her reply on her own time. I told her just to hear me out, that I could meet her wherever she wanted and I could explain everything from the beginning.

She only stated it was fine.

Fine.

How could it be fine? How could *she* be fine?

I sure as hell wasn't fine.

She told me it didn't matter. That we shouldn't have been doing what we were doing anyway, and that she would see me around.

See me around, like Joe-Schmo off the street. Like I mean so little to her.

She's just angry. She'll come around.

I keep repeating that same sentence, over and over. It's my new prayer.

I decided then, that I would give her that space. Give her a few days for the preliminary blow to wear off, then I would go to her and tell her everything. Tell her how wrong it is for us not to be with one another. She was made for me. How can she not see that?

Kennedy

I CAN BARELY SEE THROUGH the veil of unshed tears as I walk along the path I know so well. The alleyway behind Buckey's is lit just slightly by the streetlamps, giving an eerie glow to the late summer night. I hear something behind me—no, someone. I turn just in time to see a flash of bright red. I pick up my pace, racing toward my apartment as wicked laughter echoes around me. Chills break out along my spine from the unnatural sound. My boots slap against the concrete as I run, my breathing coming out in short, choppy pants.

Someone stands at the end of the road I'm on and suddenly, the faint aroma of smoke fills my nostrils.

The figure slowly comes into view. It's Palmer.

My heart warms at the sight of him. His worn blue jeans fit his figure perfectly as his sculpted thighs strain against the denim. His dark Henley, rolled up at the elbows, hugs the defined muscles rippling under the waffled fabric. I slow my run to a gait—I'm safe, nothing and no one can hurt me when Palmer is near.

The smell of smoke intensifies, searing my nostrils as I approach his side.

"What are you doing here?" I question, gazing up at his scruff-covered and chiseled jaw.

He replies, never once making eye contact with me.

"Waiting for you, Darling."

Waiting for me?

Palmer is watching something and I turn, following his gaze to a couple off in the distance.

The couple turns our direction, but their faces are contorted. I can't make out who they are. The wicked laughter grows increasingly closer, the smoke smell seemingly right upon me as the couple's disfigured faces taunt me in the distance.

"What—" Something strikes hard against my back and I fall forward, landing on the rough pavement. I grab my knee, wincing from the pain as I look up, the unknown faces hovering over me.

Palmer is gone when I look back up.

I scream, but nothing comes out.

The menacing laughter is coming from the faceless couple, and the smoke I smelled earlier is pouring out from the soles of their feet. Before I can crawl away, flames engulf the hovering bodies, the laughter growing louder, nearly piercing my eardrums.

I can't move.

I can't scream.

I close my eyes and the laughter stops. When I dare open them again, Palmer and the woman from his house appear before me, bloodied and disfigured. They were the faceless couple before me.

They close in on me and I'm frozen. I look down at their hands, clasped together before me, and darkness falls upon us, completely disorienting me.

What is going on?

"We've been waiting for you, Kennedy," the faceless duo whispers, one to either side of me now. The crescendo of sinister laughter picks up once more, growing louder and louder until the only way to drown it out is to scream at the top of my lungs and—

I shoot up, gasping for air. My bed is saturated with sweat, and the alarm clock to my left shows it's pushing three in the morning. I run a hand over my face to calm my nerves. My chest is tight. Slapping a hand over my breast, I squeeze, trying to quell the lingering pain beneath. The discomfort doesn't lessen—it only grows.

Every day, every minute, every second…it grows.

Four days without Palmer.

Four days of this—waking up in a cold sweat after the most bizarre dreams.

Each one is different, yet each one is similar.

Each time we're somewhere else, and each time he's there. With *her.*

PALMER

DAY SIX.

It's been six fucking days. That's almost a goddamn week.

At least now I've eaten some food. I'm at work today. I even showered, shaved, and smoothed my hair into submission as to not scare off the citizens of Beacon Hill. I don't look dead any longer, but I still feel it. Well, I feel nothing, really. The numbness has spread to every nerve, every crevice. Every damn atom of my being is numb. This is my life since Kennedy walked out of it.

A knock on my office door registers somewhere in my mind, but I don't bother looking up. I only stare straight ahead, the same spot I've been focused on for the last ten minutes I've been sitting here.

"Cole. Hey, man." Greg waits for me to reply to his greeting. After a moment with no response, he continues as if I had. "Dolan and I are grabbing something to eat over at Mulligan's. I would ask you to come, but I know you'll say no.

So instead, I'm telling you to get your ass up because you're coming with. We're leaving in five." He raps his hand twice on the doorframe. My stomach betrays me and rumbles at the mention of food. Greg smiles knowingly and I simply nod once.

At least Kennedy won't be there seeing me like this.

We pull up to Mulligan's Pub and it's packed.

Great.

As we ascend the stairs to the building, Dolan and Greg are in a heated debate over gas versus charcoal grilling. I've tuned out all of the conversation up until I hear my name.

"Right, Palmer? I mean, it's no contest." Dolan looks at me expectantly, so I decide to appease him.

"Sure. No contest."

No fucking clue what I just agreed to.

"I Like Me Better" is playing overhead and I almost lose it. I'm holding on by a thread as it is, and then this shit decides to taunt me.

Dolan and Greg resume their debate while the hostess looks at me, asking how many are in our party. I hold three fingers out at waist level, grateful for not having to engage in more conversation. She happily weaves us through the congested bar area into the back room where the dining area is. Halfway through the excursion to our table, I see her and my stomach churns.

Kennedy is here.

Wait, Kennedy is here? It must be a mirage. A beautiful,

cruel joke of a mirage. I'm dehydrated and seeing things. It's the only logical answer.

"Shit, buddy." Greg walks straight into my back, not realizing I've stopped dead in my tracks, and braces himself on my biceps. "What are you looking—oh. *Damn*."

I must not be seeing things; he can see her too.

She really is here.

Heat ripples through my body at the realization of being so near to her. Every. Single. Part of me is itching to run to her, but she hasn't seen me yet. I use these few moments of reprieve to soak her in. Her long hair is down, flowing around her back in the beachy way I love. The blond and silver strands shine under the overhead light. She's wearing minimal makeup and still looks like a fucking model. Her denim shorts leave little to the imagination, showing off her toned legs, which are crossed at her boot covered ankles. Her tight black tank top bares her inked skin. She's giving every red-blooded male in this place quality spank bank material for life.

"Let's just order a pizza, man. We'll head back to my place, throw on a game, and drink some beers. C'mon." Dolan tries to steer me out of the pub by my shoulder, turning my body just so that I finally take notice of who Kennedy is here with.

What little is left of my heart stops beating, my vision begins to blur, and a sharp static like buzzing commences between my ears.

Because with her, is *fucking Spencer*…and his hand is on hers.

CHAPTER TWENTY-TWO

Kennedy

GOD, I DON'T WANT TO be here with him.

For the second time this week...I'm a stupid girl. These past six days have been a living nightmare, a kind of pain I wouldn't inflict on my worst enemy. In a moment of weakness, and also to get him to stop asking, I agreed to get dinner with Spencer. I told him strictly as friends, which apparently means the exact opposite in his mind.

"This winter, Rebecca Moore's father is letting her use their camp in Vancouver, and we're going skiing for a few nights. I'll be able to teach you how to ski—get you all sweaty on the slopes before we get sweaty in the sack." His mischievous wink makes me nauseous, and I regret ever agreeing to this.

Maybe if you bash your head off the table hard enough, you'll black out and be escorted off the premises by ambulance.

Sucking in a sharp breath, I let it out slowly and finish off the rest of my water. "You promised you wouldn't do this. I only agreed to come with you as a *friend*. This isn't a date, or us getting back together. If I knew you were going to pull this shit—" I struggle to get out of the booth, but his hand lands on mine, halting my departure.

"Look, I'm sorry." He licks his lips and it's reptilian, reminding me of a predator waiting for its next meal. "I've got it bad for you, you know this. Not being able to have the one thing I want, when I want it, isn't something I'm used to." He rubs his thumb along the side of my hand, still underneath his. "Just hard to control myself around you."

I don't typically have sympathy for people who treat others like they're their property, or beneath them. Spencer is no exception.

"*Spencer...*" I say through gritted teeth, closing my eyes briefly to contain the scream about to erupt. I should be home, sprawled out on my couch wearing pajamas, watching gory movies and eating my weight in pistachio ice cream.

"The more you fight it, the more I want you," Spencer says, shrugging, his head cocked slightly to the side almost studying me. "Every chick in this town and back at school, they throw themselves at me. The one girl I want..." He trails off and laughs humorlessly under his breath, shaking his head in annoyance. "I could give you everything you've ever wanted."

I know this. I know that he could. He has more money than he knows what to do with.

But he still isn't what I want.

That's because he's not a six-foot-three mechanic with magic fingers and emerald eyes...

Underneath his pretty boy features, he's just...not good. I've tried before to think otherwise, but all in all Spencer Laurent is a mind-numbingly cliché character taken from a bad romantic comedy. The rich bad boy offering the sad, lost girl the world. I need *more*. I know I need more than good looks and bottomless bank accounts. Living in a world where I've felt the adoration of Cole Palmer; moneybags here is simply uninspiring at best.

I internally slap myself. I know I can't keep romanticizing our time together. Palmer is married. He never was and never will be mine. I need to just accept that. The only problem is…I can't seem to shake him. Even now, thinking of him, I feel that electric buzz, the burn I feel whenever he's near.

It's almost like—*no, it can't be.*

But I feel him.

Out of my peripheral, I see a figure making their way toward our table quite…briskly.

As I turn to get a better look, I lock eyes with the reason my heart has been shattered into a million tiny pieces.

"What the fuck do you think you're doing here, Colson?" Spencer's words drip venom. "We're a little busy here."

Wait. What? Colson?

I find myself instinctively pulling my hand back into my lap.

"I need to talk to you." Palmer doesn't even acknowledge Spencer's question, nor his presence. His eyes penetrate the deepest parts of me. "Please, Ken. Let me explain."

I can only stare up at him, but my insides betray me and liquify, his low voice turning me to mush.

Spencer exits the booth, standing nearly chest to chest with Palmer, although with his shorter stature, his head barely meets the top of Palmer's shoulders. "Are you going deaf in your old age? I said, what the *fuck* are you doing here?" He gives a shove to Palmer's chest and the hair on the back of my neck stands up. *No, no, no, no…*I hop up out of my seat. The entire pub is about to catch onto the exchange taking place here if I don't separate these two.

"I heard you just fine. I chose not to waste my goddamn breath. I'm here for one thing, and I'm not leaving until I speak with my girl."

My girl. My heart involuntarily flutters.

Palmer looks at me, sadness prevalent in those green eyes I miss so damn much. "I just need a minute."

"Like hell you do." Spencer puffs up his chest. "She's with me. This bullshit little fantasy you created with her is just that...a *fantasy*. It's a fucking joke. She's not interested in your stupi—"

I see it coming, but before I can stop it, Palmer's fist makes direct contact with Spencer's nose. The crack of bone on bone echoes throughout the room, only dimmed slightly by the overhead music as the gasps and hushed voices make their way around the room. I rush between the two men before it can go any further, angling my back to Spencer's front. Facing Palmer, I press my palm flush against his heaving chest. My pleading eyes search his as his harsh breaths begin to even out. The fluttering beneath my hand simmers and the snarl on his face smooths into submission. I look down where his fist was clenched a moment ago, and see it relaxed. Content that he won't fly off the handle, I turn to survey the damage to Spencer's face before someone decides to call the police. Spencer is hunched forward, holding on to his face while a thin line of blood trickles down his forearm. The sight is oddly comical and I have to choke down the laughter threatening to escape.

"You're gonna pay for that, motherfucker." He seethes through gritted teeth, wiping his bloodied nose with the back of his hand. "I hope you enjoyed your butt buddies from prison, 'cause I'm sending your worthless ass back there where you fucking belong." The hatred in his normally ice blue eyes shines clear as day, turning them a deep cobalt, and I know what I have to do—the only thing I can to get him not to resort to legal action against Palmer.

"Come on." I grab ahold of Spencer's arm, attempting to leave, only to have him stay rooted in place. With another forceful tug, I get him to walk with me begrudgingly. With just a look, I silently plead with Palmer to let us walk out of here and not cause a bigger scene. He can't go back to jail over me. I wouldn't survive losing another person so indefinitely, especially him. I toss a few bills on the table to cover our drinks and appetizer. As we walk toward him, I silently mouth *I'll come to you.*

Palmer looks down at the ground, outwardly defeated as we shoulder past him.

PALMER

I CAN'T BREATHE. THE AIR has been completely sucked out of the room. I'm suffocating; bleeding out as Kennedy takes the last shattered pieces of my heart with her. She mouthed something to me, what appeared to be *how could you?* I couldn't bear to look at her any longer, choosing to stare at the floor, willing the ground to part and Hell to take me home.

Too late. You're already fucking there.

Spencer stops short just next to me as they pass, our shoulders pressed against one another as he leans up to speak.

"Isn't it funny," he says just loud enough into my ear that

only I can hear him. "You're practically old enough to be her father, but I'm the one she's gonna be calling *daddy* tonight." My head whips to the side to face him as I clench my fists to avoid snapping his neck like a goddamn twig. His sinister smile taunts me as he licks the blood from his teeth and continues out of Mulligan's with my entire world attached to his arm.

I stand where she left me, shattered and confused. Why would she leave with him? She fucking hates him.

Or that's just what she wanted you to think…

Dolan and Greg circle around me from each side. I know they're speaking to me, but I can't quite make out the words. All I do know is they lead me out of the pub, all surrounding eyes on me as we exit.

Yeah, keep staring. The town fuckup strikes again. Soak it all in, fuckers.

Only once I'm in the dark backseat of the truck, leaning my head against the headrest do I allow my tears to flow. Silent salt lines leak from the corners of my eyes, pooling in the hollows of my ears.

How did everything get so fucked? This time last week I was balls deep in the only woman I've ever truly loved, and now she's walking away for good, attached to the spawn of Satan himself.

I need a goddamn drink.

CHAPTER TWENTY-THREE

Kennedy

STRANGERS STARE AS I DRAG Spencer, bloody and cursing, out the door by the crook of his arm. No doubt witnessing the scene inside and wanting to know what happens next.

When did my life become a soap opera?

"That piece of shit, I swear to God. He's gonna regret this," Spencer continues smearing the blood dripping from his nose on the back of his hand. Looking down at his blood-covered shirt, he turns to me with wide eyes. "How bad is it? I mean it, if he fucked up my face…I'll fucking end him. He needs to be back behind bars. He's a goddamn *animal!*"

Looking at the state of his shirt and the blood that has made its way out of his facial cavity to the back of his arm, you would think there was a murder back there. I know that head wounds bleed more than other areas, so I'm not quite as concerned as Spencer seems to be. He'll bruise—but he'll live.

"He wasn't exactly an animal…*per se*…I mean, you did provoke him."

Spencer halts as we reach his souped-up Tesla. Turning

to face me, he leans in, so close I can nearly count the individual pores on his swollen face.

"I *what?*" He seethes through his clenched jaw—I don't think his face has left that compressed state since he was on the receiving end of Palmer's fist five minutes ago. "Are you seriously defending that criminal?"

I scoff at his word choice. "He isn't a *criminal*, Spencer. He was defending his sister before and you pushed him first tonight. You can't send him back over *that*. I'll testify that's how it happened if I have to…no one is going to fucking prison over this."

He merely stares at me.

"You'll testify on his behalf? I think you've been watching too many shitty TV shows there, Darling." He laughs humorlessly and attempts to open his driver's side door, stopping short just before getting in. "Wait just a goddamn minute."

I freeze at his chilling tone. I've already made my way to the passenger side with my door swung open. His elbows rest on the roof of the car, and his eyes turn to slits as he peers over at me with disdain.

"You're talking like someone—nah, you can't be—you're not *in love with him*, are you?" The realization, or maybe it's disbelief in his voice, is prevalent.

When I can't answer him, I glance down at my feet briefly before steeling my reserve and turning back to face him. His eyes widen impossibly large and he lets out the evilest cackle I've ever heard. My hair stands on end.

"You are! You're in love with that fucking guy! How did I not see that before?" He rakes his non-blood-covered hand through his short blond hair wildly, pulling at the roots. "No wonder you won't get back with me. It seems I'm no longer your type." His eyes look me up and down with revulsion.

"You prefer them aged with criminal backgrounds."

"Enough with all the criminal shit, Spencer!" I slam the passenger side door shut. "Jesus. Yes, okay? I do. I love him. I have for a while and we kept it a secret so people like *you* in this town couldn't judge us for it." His laughter grows louder behind me as I turn to walk away, ordering an Uber to take me home to get my car.

"You'll regret this, Kennedy! Mark my fucking words. I'm taking that fucker down and you with him if I have to!" His voice is laced with hatred and his shouting causes more eyes to look in our direction.

I should be worried. This is exactly what I wanted to avoid when I moved here. Drama. People talking about my life, just like before. Complications. I shouldn't be thinking about anything other than keeping my head down, working my ass off, and bettering my life. Instead, all I can think about is getting back to Palmer.

I sprint inside to grab my car keys the second the Uber drops me off at home. I pause in front of the mirror in my entryway to inspect my outfit. Why I'm worried about how I look when I'm only planning to get answers out of Palmer is beyond me. I call his cell several times with no answer.

The drive to his house goes quickly; because of my increased speed or racing thoughts, I can't be sure. I lay down rubber with an abrupt stop in his driveway and barely have time to shut the door before I'm racing up the front porch, pounding my fist against the wooden entrance.

Nothing.

I slam my hand onto the porch railing, reveling in the sting it leaves behind as I hop back into my car.

Where is he? I told him I would come find him. Why is he not here?

Maybe he doesn't want to see me. I know I left with Spencer, but I told him I would come to him. I'm giving *him* the chance to explain. I don't understand. I try his number again and still nothing.

Wracking my brain, I think of all the places Palmer might be. He wouldn't go to the shop this late. Maybe his sister's house, although I don't have the slightest clue where that is. All I do know is nearly an hour has passed since we left the pub; Palmer could be at JFK on his way to Cuernavaca for all I know.

No, he wouldn't leave his family without saying something to one of them.

That's it. *Travis.* Dialing his nephews' number, I'm pleased to hear his voice after only two rings.

"Hey, Kennedy…what's up?"

"Travis! Hey, is your uncle there with you by any chance?" I'm internally pleading with a God I don't believe in to let him be there with them.

"Nah, I haven't seen him today."

My heart plummets.

Where the hell is he?

"Why? What's going on?"

"Nothing major," I lie. "Just need to speak with him."

"Sorry, Ken, I have no idea where he might be. I'm not sure where people his age go to hang out. It's not like he's a clubber." He chuckles.

Then it hits me like a TKO. *Elixir.*

"No worries. Thanks anyway, Trav." I attempt to hang up without waiting for a reply, but then a thought occurs to me. "Uh, actually, I have a few questions for you…"

I back out of Palmer's driveway and head south. It's going to take me at least forty-five minutes to get there, so I might as well get some answers.

I hope I'm right about this.

Finding parking this time around isn't quite as easy as it was with Palmer the first night I came here. I manage to snag a spot about five blocks away and I press the key fob nearly fifty times, assuring that I've locked my car doors as I sprint my way to the main entrance. Out of breath, heartbroken and frantic, I easily weave my way to the front of the line and recognize the bouncer from a few weeks back.

"Hey, hi, remember me? With Cole Palmer? He told me to just head in after him." I give the chiseled mammoth of a man my best smile. He slowly steps aside with a raised eyebrow and I slide by and mouth a silent *thank you* to my new accomplice.

I scan the crowd while Maria Brink's raspy voice blares all around me from the speakers, singing about a big bad wolf. The bass reverberates in my chest, fueling me forward through the sea of bodies.

I realize now why Palmer held on to me so tight the last time we were here, almost as if he was shielding me. There are eyes on me everywhere I look. Men gawking at me like I'm a piece of meat—they're the lions out for blood and I'm the gazelle. Suddenly I'm rethinking my plan in coming here alone.

I just need to find Palmer, and then everything will be fine.

I push my way forward, remembering the setup from before; the women on the poles in the front of the room, the DJ booth, the bar to my right and the dance floor in front of me. I don't peg Palmer for a dancer, so the center of the room is out. I make my way to the bar, hoping to find him nursing a drink or at least the bartender from last time. A hand grasping onto my upper arm halts my advance, and I let out a sigh of relief that he found me. Only, when I turn, the man who has me in his throngs isn't anyone I recognize.

"I see you're lookin' for someone. I think you might have just found him," he coos in my ear, much too close for my liking. I attempt to back away, but his vice grip on my arm stays firm.

"Uh, no actually…I'm meeting a f-friend here…my boyfriend? Cole Palm—"

Instantly this mystery man releases me and backs away, palms facing outward.

"*Shit*, sorry, sweetheart. I didn't know you were with Colson. He's over there." His long index finger points over my shoulder at a corner of the warehouse I didn't get to see last time, which is blocked off by large curtains. "Honestly, if I knew you were his, I wouldn't have—just, *shit*." Mystery man disappears into the sea of bodies on the dance floor.

Uh, what the hell just happened?

Shaking off the worrisome encounter, I make my way over to the corner of the room he told me Palmer was in. My heart is lodged in my throat, beating away at full speed. I pull back the sheer wine-colored curtain, and a gasp sneaks its way from between my lips. This room is filled with plush leather couches, and fancy recliners—all in use. Bodies gyrating on one another it seems. Lap dances? Public…sex room? *Orgies*?

God, I am so out of my depth, here. What is this and why would Palmer be back here?

I scan the crowd before me, looking for my muscled and tattooed target, and finally see him. He's laughing, and I let out a fleeting sigh of relief. He isn't alone like I am—the topless blonde bouncing up and down on his lap assures me of that fact.

CHAPTER TWENTY-FOUR

PALMER

PATHETIC.

I am the most pathetic man I know. Reduced to getting drunk by myself, nearly bawling my eyes out while getting a lap dance from a decent-looking woman with great tits. I scoff at the state of myself, and the nameless woman on my lap turns to look at me over her shoulder.

"You say something, handsome?" The slight southern drawl to her voice turns me off. I can't even pretend this woman is who I want her to be—she sounds wrong.

This is all wrong.

I don't even bother answering her. I just grunt in her general direction. Thankfully, she takes the hint and continues her gyrations against my groin.

I can't even get hard. What the actual fuck is wrong with me?

I guess it could be all the liquor I consumed in the last hour. Whiskey dick is a *real* thing. I close my eyes and lean my head back against the leather couch I'm seated on. My mind drifts to Kennedy.

Always to Kennedy.

I imagine her silver-blond waves cascading down her toned back, her tight, lithe body with that intricate ink I love so much, her smart mouth, and those nearly ever-present combat boots. *Those damn boots.* I almost chuckle at the memory of her tiny body parading around in such heavy things. My heart warms, much like the rest of my body from the liquor, at the memories of my hazel-eyed girl. This time, when I pry my lids apart, I can almost pretend the blond waves bouncing in front of me belong to Kennedy. I perk up for a moment, but once my eyes focus, I see the color is all wrong. It's too platinum, too *different.* I miss the silver strands on my favorite girl. I find myself chuckling even though nothing about the situation is even remotely funny. Alcohol does strange things to people during emotional times.

Simply at the thought of her, my heart constricts and tears brim my eyes. I lost my chance, and now fucking Spencer has his claws sunk into her flesh again.

She's gone.

From the corner of my eye, movement and a small gasp catch my attention and I swear I see a blurry silhouette of Kennedy through the wall of tears building in my eyes, threatening to spill over. The thought only makes me laugh harder. I'm a drunk, grown-ass man, *crying* while getting a lap dance, pining over a twenty-two-year-old girl who wants nothing to do with me.

They should make a TV show out of the train wreck that is my life. It'd be a hit.

My eyes close once again, my lids proving to be heavier than I would like, and I hear steps approaching over the blaring electronic beat of "Scars" by Basement Jaxx.

"We need to talk. *Now.*" That voice. It sounds so far away and yet so close at the same time. *Am I dreaming?* My heavy lids flutter, and I'm pleading my subconscious to repeat the voice. I need to hear that delicious, honey-sweet sound again.

"*Colson Palmer*…did you hear me? I said, we are leaving. Let's go."

Colson? Kennedy has never called me by my full name; I never even told her that. *How would she know that?* Now I know I'm dreaming. I feel a rough tug on my arm, and I flinch, standing abruptly and dizzily to my feet. The sudden change in position sends the nameless blonde toppling off my lap onto the floor on her hands and knees. My drunken stupor causes me to bust out laughing instead of helping the poor girl up.

"Shit, my bad." I laugh, shaking the fogginess from my brain. The blonde scampers off, scowling and completely unimpressed with the turn of events. Still laughing, I turn my attention toward the hand on my forearm. Black lines meld together, drawing my eyes up the length of my intruder's arm until my sight lands on the most beautiful face.

Kennedy?

For the second time tonight, it's not a mirage. If I hadn't already been crying, the sheer reprieve I feel from having her here with me would cripple me with tears of relief. I weasel my arm from her grasp and frame her angelic face between my large hands.

My voice comes out as a whisper, muffled more so by the loud music blaring throughout the club. "You're real." Her confused stare has me questioning what I just said out loud. My mind is foggy, clouded by too much liquor. I'm not sure of anything right now.

"Real as can be, Romeo. Now let's go, you are *so* drunk. I have my car. We can figure out how to get yours back tomorrow." She leads me by the wrist, quite roughly I might add, through the curtains and into the main bar area. I tip my chin to the bartender, my friend Becks, as I pass by. Her amused face is shadowed by the dim light in the area. I see all the men in our vicinity gawking at Kennedy. My blood gelatinizes in my veins and my fists clench.

She's mine.

The looks continue and I fear I may cause a scene with all the testosterone coursing through my system. Skirting in front of Kennedy, I see them notice, one by one, that she's with me. Their looks seem to evade us as we part through the sea of bodies like Moses. My chest puffs up.

Yeah, that's what I fucking thought.

I lead us through the masses and onto the street. The air is cooler out here, and I breathe deep, standing still and filling my lungs with the crisp air.

"You can smell the roses later, *Slater*, it's time to go." Kennedy gives another rough tug on my arm, pulling me into the present as I scramble to keep pace with her.

Who knew those little legs of hers could move so quickly?

"If I'm A.C Slater does that make you Jessie?" I laugh at the whole thing; Kennedy referencing *Saved by the Bell*, which is older than she is, and her five-foot-two self personally dragging my drunken ass out of a sex club.

"Keep it up and I'll be calling you Screech with your drunk ass. How much have you had to drink tonight, anyway? You can barely walk, Palmer!"

How much have I had? That's a good question.

"Somewhere between a lot and a lot more." I chuckle, apparently finding it more amusing than she does, since I'm met with an unimpressed stare. "I lost count after nearly a bottle of Jameson," I admit somberly, lifting my shoulders to my ears and then dropping them dramatically.

Kennedy only shakes her head. "Get in."

We somehow made it to her car in record time, those speedy legs of hers carrying us along much faster than I anticipated. She lets go of my forearm to circle around her side of the vehicle, and the loss of contact hurts worse than I expect it to. I hunker down into Kennedy's tiny sedan, my long legs cramped between the seat and the dash, and the apologies begin spilling out before she even has time to put the key in the ignition.

"Look, it's not what you think, I jus—"

"Stop, just…wait, please." She cuts me off, staring straight ahead, refusing to look at me. "We need to have a serious talk, and I don't think it is the best time to have it while you're plastered. Sober up some on the drive home and then we'll talk. I'm driving to your place." Like a child scolded by their mother, I do as I'm told and sit silently in the passenger seat. My alcohol-fogged brain is having a hard time focusing on one thing at a time, so it's probably best that I don't speak for a while anyway.

The heavy-lidded sensation washes over me once more and I have to fight to keep my eyes open. Stretching my arm across the center console, I rest my palm against Kennedy's smooth thigh. I feel her tense at first and then she noticeably relaxes. I let the comfort of her soft, warm skin against my hand push me off the edge as I free fall into a liquid-induced slumber.

I peel open my eyes to see Kennedy leaning above me, coaxing me awake with a tentative palm on my cheek.

"We're here. Wake up," she whispers gently, to which I'm thankful since the effects of the alcohol coursing through my system have worn off significantly, and now a brutal migraine is rearing its ugly head. I groan when the overhead light pops on signaling an open door. I shield my eyes from the piercing brightness and feel Kennedy move away, exiting the vehicle. I do the same and meet her at my front door, thankfully able to walk myself steadily. I probe the knob a few times, missing the mark with each attempt before Kennedy grabs the key from me and allows us inside. Locking the door behind her, she drops her purse and the keys onto the table in the entryway. I snag her now free hand and attempt to lead her up the stairs to my bedroom.

I need sleep.

"No, no, no, we are *talking*." She digs her heels in. Stubborn little one she is. "Neutral rooms only."

"Neutral room? We've fucked in my living room, every surface in my kitchen, my dining room, both of my bathrooms, and even that one time in my laundry room through a spin cycle." I thicken at the memory. "Which room do you suggest we have this little chat in?" I quirk an eyebrow and she sighs, leading me by the hand into the living room.

She seats herself with a *plunk*, and I follow suit right next to her, pulling my leg up so I can face her on the couch. I place both palms on either cheek before she can object, pressing my lips to her forehead. Her body gives up some of its resistance as she melts into my embrace. I breathe in her peach scent a moment longer before I sit upright, begrudgingly letting go of her beautiful face.

"Do you have anything you want to say, or can I explain? From the beginning, I promise." I search her eyes for any signs of doubt but come up lacking.

She nods at me to continue, placing her hand on my knee, giving me the courage I didn't know I needed.

"Amber and I." I sigh. "We got together five years ago. She was a couple years behind me in school, and I honestly never gave her the time of day back then—I just wasn't ever interested, you know? Then one day, it was as if she grew up overnight, she was so pretty, and seemed so sure of herself; what she wanted out of life. I guess it drew me in. We were good together for the first year of our relationship, or so I thought." I let out a breath and take in Kennedy's beautifully delicate features, urging myself to carry on with my tale. "What I didn't know is how good of an actress she was. Not until much later, anyway. We got married shortly after she told me she was pregnant. Thinking that was the next step, we had a little ceremony and prepared to be a small family of three—but the baby girl never came. She had lied about everything." The small intake of breath that leaves Kennedy's parted lips presses me forward.

"Shortly after I found out there was no baby, I got sent away, as you already know. While I was gone, I discovered that Amber had been sending illicit photos of herself to…" I stop myself. Kennedy's eyes are wide, expectant, and waiting for what I'm about to tell her.

"She was sending photos to Spencer. They were carrying on behind my back, thinking I would never find out. When they released me, I made sure to break things off with her. We are one hundred percent separated in all the ways that matter, Kennedy, I swear to you. It's not official through the courts yet, since that stuff takes time and I hadn't been out all that long before you came into the picture and I've been a little…*preoccupied* since, to say the least." This earns me a chuckle. "Amber has been out of my life officially since I found out about the baby and then the two of them going on like they did solidified that. I haven't touched another woman or considered the idea since I knew I was in love with you months ago. I mean, tonight was a close call, but I didn't touch that dancer. I swear. I couldn't even get hard for a half-naked chick in my lap." I allow myself to snicker at the absurdity of it all, resting my head back on the couch.

"I know."

Her confession makes me straighten and I pause, waiting for her to go on.

"I asked Travis tonight what the situation was with you and Amber. He explained that it was past tense. I just needed to hear you say it out loud."

The hard expression on her face softens marginally, and her eyes drop to where my leg is pressed into her thigh. Her molten gaze slowly rises to meet mine again, and she does the last thing I expect her to as her lips find mine. Fireworks explode behind my eyelids. All synapses in my body are firing hot, warming me from the inside out. Her mouth tastes exquisite, and it feels so right with our bodies melding this way. Nothing has ever felt more right. I force myself to pull back just far enough to look her in the eyes.

I just need to know one thing.

"Please tell me you didn't sleep with him while we've been apart." I hold my breath for her response, not sure I can bear to hear her say the words.

"I didn't." She shakes her head. "I haven't...been with anyone since you. Well, since the time in my apartment you were there for. I couldn't. I can't seem to shake you. It's like you're embedded in my soul." She laughs and I find myself amused along with her, and our kisses resume, turning to quickening pecks. Her lips touching my cheeks, my neck and then back up.

Heaven.

"Trust me, babe." I tuck a tendril of loose hair behind her ear. "I'm right there with you."

Kennedy pulls herself up to her knees on the couch and swings a leg over my lap, straddling me, as I situate us more comfortably.

"So, *Colson*, anything else you need to explain to me before I take my clothes off?" Her eyebrow is raised in a taunt, so I know she doesn't hate me—*finally*. I allow myself my first genuine laugh since she walked out of my life six days ago.

"About that." I crack my neck from side to side as she pecks a kiss on alternating sides as I go. "My full name is Colson Palmer. I started going by Cole once I got out of prison. That shit tends to leave a smear on your reputation. I thought it might cut down some on the side chatter. Apparently, I was wrong." We both laugh in unison, and I pull her mouth down to meet mine once again. "Now, about these clothes coming off…"

CHAPTER TWENTY-FIVE

Kennedy

PALMER'S MUSCLES FLEX AND CONTRACT as he bends with his chest lifted and his back straight, deadlifting nearly three times my body weight. The repeated motion, up, down, up, down has me drooling.

It should be illegal to be this attractive.

As I'm finishing my third mile on the elliptical, my phone begins dancing in the cup holder, signaling a phone call. *Mother Dearest* reads on the display. I groan, definitely not hiding my distaste for the woman who birthed me. I wish I could be one of those girls who enjoys calling their mother, getting advice on boys and talking about nails and fun girly things. Unfortunately, I've never had that type of relationship with mine. Especially since she blames me for everything wrong in her life. I'm sure if she broke a nail tomorrow, somehow it would be my fault.

I continue with my workout, simply slowing my strides down to a slow gait. Knowing she'll just continue to call if I don't answer, I pick up the call.

"Hello, Mother."

"Kennedy. You could seem a bit more enthusiastic when I call. I am your mother after all."

I sigh. "I'm at the gym. This is about all the enthusiasm I can muster this morning. Everything...okay?"

Not that I care.

"Everything is *fine*, Kennedy. Can't a mother call her *only* child without there being something wrong?" She loves reminding me of that fact. "I mean, really." Her shrill voice grates on my nerves already and the call isn't even sixty seconds in.

"Of course you can, Ma, I'm just...making sure." My expression must be telling. That or my eyes rolling into the back of my head pique Palmer's interest. He walks over to me with a questioning look on his face, wiping the sweat from his furrowed brow with the bottom of his shirt. I move the phone away from my mouth and quietly explain that it's my mother. His tongue finds the space between his top teeth and gums as he nods curtly—clearly unimpressed with the news. He's received the abridged version of my relationship with her, and it's safe to say that he's *not* a fan.

"What? Who are you speaking to?"

I bring the phone back to my lips.

"Hello? Kennedy!"

"Sorry, Mom, I was speaking to Palmer. We're at the gym. Like I already said."

"Palmer? Who is *Palmer*?" She says his name like it's a curse word. "Why does that name sound familiar?"

"I'm not sure why it would," I say. "He's my boyfriend." I don't even realize what I've said until after the words slip from my tongue. The word bounces around the enclosed gym like a ping-pong ball. Palmer's eyes widen and a blindingly white smile flashes in my direction. It's not as if she would ever meet him anyway, so her opinion on the matter is non-existent. I match his smile; thankful his look isn't one of disgust. I wait for the shocked pause on the other end of the receiver to turn to yelling, but to my surprise, the yelling never comes.

"Interesting." She says the word slowly. "Well, in any news, that brings me to the reason for my call. I will be flying in next week. Lars has business there and I will be accompanying him on this trip. If your schedule is packed, please clear it and make time to meet me. See you soon." The line goes dead.

Not how I was imagining that going.

I tip my head back in annoyance and let out a groan. I need at least a month to emotionally prepare before my mother's arrival. A few days is not nearly enough. When I open my eyes and face Palmer once again, he's still trained on me with a look I've never seen before in his eyes.

"Your boyfriend, huh?" His tone is unreadable.

I look away, slightly embarrassed by my use of the juvenile term. We've never spoken about labels or what to call this thing we're doing; we've always just been Kennedy and Palmer. *Us.* My discomfort continues to grow, not knowing how to reply. I take a deep breath and turn my head back to him, braving a glance. To my disbelief, the large smile he had moments ago is still there. He's beaming.

"That kind of just...slipped out." I shrug, hopping off the cardio machine. "I hope that didn't make you uncomfortable. We don't need to—" I'm unable to finish my sentence before Palmer's mouth crashes into mine, his swollen, sweaty muscles enveloping me tightly. This kiss is all-consuming, and I'm thankful he has such a tight hold on me, as my legs would be sure to give out otherwise. His hot tongue laps at my mouth, dancing between my teeth and stroking along the roof of my mouth, tasting every inch.

His palms grasp onto my backside as he breaks the blissful kiss, not caring that we're in the middle of a packed gym, and we both pull away panting.

"Palmer, oh my God." I chuckle almost breathlessly.

He snickers, smiling down at me. "I will gladly answer to all three, baby." My questioning look has his ever-present smirk back in its rightful place.

"Palmer, boyfriend, and my new favorite…God." He counts off all three with his fingers and flexes as I laugh along, shaking my head at this strange man of mine. My cheeks hurt from the utter joy this conversation brings. "Does this mean I get to introduce you to the world as my girl?"

I peck a kiss to his scruff-covered cheek. "Like you haven't been already?"

Palmer swats at my ass playfully and ushers me out of the cardio room.

Exiting the gym hand in hand, for once it seems like nothing could possibly go wrong.

CHAPTER TWENTY-SIX

PALMER

THE SMILE PLASTERED ON MY face has yet to wane as we drive down the road, windows down enjoying the beautiful late August day. Kennedy's hair is pulled back into a high ponytail, exposing her slender neck. The sweat glistening on her forehead from today's workout is drying with the wind. Her eyes are closed tight, her head is back, and she's breathing in the fresh air and summer smells—all the while my eyes are trained on her. That sight far more beautiful than any summer day.

Slowing to a stop at a red light, my hard-on from our little make-out session at the gym still strains against my briefs. I rub the heel of my hand against the bulge, attempting to soothe the throbbing ache, but I only succeed in waking up the beast inside. He claws within me to get out. I grow impossibly harder. Looking back over at Kennedy, her eyes still closed in peacefulness, a thought springs to mind.

"Baby?"

She rolls her head to look at me.

"Take off your shorts and panties," I order.

Her eyes widen as she sits up straight, a smile threatening her lips.

"*What?*"

My grip on the steering wheel tightens, as the space remaining in the front of my shorts gets smaller. We're only about twenty minutes from the house, but my hunger for my girl cannot wait. I need my fix. Other cars may surround us, but we sit up high enough in my truck and the windows have just enough tint to give us some privacy.

"Do it."

The light turns green and I make my way into the intersection, while out of the corner of my eye I see Kennedy oblige, her shorts and panties falling to the floor.

That's my girl.

My gaze glides up her toned thighs, tanned and gorgeous from the summer sun. I lay my right hand on that delicious chunk of skin, making my way up to her soft and completely smooth pussy. The second my fingers graze her silky, wet skin, she sucks in a breath and my cock jumps at the sound.

"Spread your legs, baby, let me in."

She does as she's told and situates herself in the seat, spreading her legs for me.

"Wider," I demand. Shifting in my seat and leaning in just enough to keep my eyes on the road while still reaching the spot I need access to, I slowly insert two fingers, curling just a bit as I retreat them. Her fingernails dig into the flesh of my arm, clinging to me and lifting herself into each thrust—the stinging bite her nails leave only adds to the sensations. The light up ahead turns red and I slow to another stop. I shift my free hand down to my groin, cupping my length over my shorts, tugging just slightly to give myself some reprieve. I growl, rubbing my fingers faster between her thighs as the light turns green yet again.

I drive into her, pulsing my fingers as far as they can reach from this angle, and then retreat, repeating the same motions as I coax out her orgasm. Kennedy is helping me, her hand back in its same spot digging into my flesh, pulling my fingers into her clenched pussy and dancing for me, rolling her hips into my hand. From this angle, the heel of my palm is grinding against her clit and I continuously rub over her nub.

She explodes around me with a sharp cry. My fingers never relent, only pumping faster, drawing out her experience. Her insides clench around my fingers, pulsating with each ebb of her orgasm ripping through her system. Her back begins to arch and her eyes are scrunched tight—ecstasy clear as day in her expression. I let her buck against my fingers until she slumps down into the seat, legs splayed open, and her chest heaving from exertion. Her hooded eyes reach mine from across the front seat. Her harsh breathing eases, but my panting can be heard over the stereo, "Flagpole Sitta" by Harvey Danger serenading us. Her chuckle resounds in the space between us and I look up to find her licking her lips.

"I like you bossy," she chirps, biting down on her bottom lip. "If I attempt to take care of your"—she waves her finger toward my groin— "*problem*, are we gonna go off the road?"

The thought of getting road head from this girl nearly pushes me over the edge, but we are close enough to the house that I think I can hold off for a few more minutes.

I tug her lip out from between her teeth and move my hand to cradle her cheek, stroking my thumb along her smooth skin.

"Probably." I laugh. "Give yourself a few minutes to recover, because once we're in that house, we're not leaving. I'm going to be so deep in your throat, your tonsils and I are gonna be best friends before the night is over."

The squeak that escapes her lips amuses me, and I turn up the volume, racing toward our destination.

We don't leave my bedroom once.

CHAPTER TWENTY-SEVEN

Kennedy

"WE ARE *SO* OVERDUE FOR a party. I won't take no for an answer, so you better get coverage for work and tell that man of yours that you are *mine* for the night." Sterling's excited tone has me almost looking forward to a girls' night. I've been spending most of my free time with Palmer, and I don't want to be one of those girls who ditch their best friend when they begin dating. Or seeing each other? Bleh, it sounds so strange when it's worded that way. Palmer and I are…*Palmer and I.* The boyfriend title only slipped out a few days ago, so the label still feels foreign to me.

"Okay, okay." I laugh. "You twisted my arm. Help me pick out my outfit." Sterling squeals and pounces into makeover mode. I shoot a text off to Jim asking for the night off, to which he quickly replies to go out and have fun.

Sterling pulls out a tight, sheer black bodycon suit with a deep V-neck from her closet and tosses it on the bed. Next are a pair of skin-tight faux leather pants and a pair of black heels with red soles. I eye them suspiciously.

"They're used—I'm not a rich, bitch." She laughs,

guessing my thoughts, and turns her back to her closet to begin selecting her own outfit. I snag the items off the bed and start changing, peeling the pants up my legs like a second skin. Thank God we're the same size.

"Uh, Sterling…" I whine mid-change. "I can't wear a bra with this."

She smirks, still searching through her closet.

"That's kind of the point, babe. When you're well-endowed, ya gotta show 'em off!"

Slithering into the top that could pass as body paint, I turn to survey the damage.

"Jesus, Sterl, you can see my nipple rings through this top!"

She turns to face me and whistles.

"Work it, girl!" She pretends to whip a lasso above her head and grabs at her crotch like a perverted man. I can't help but laugh at her. "Seriously…that outfit is *hot* on you. Toss on your signature smoky eye and we'll have to fight the guys off you tonight." She winks.

That's not exactly what I'm going for…

Seeing my expression, she quickly adds, "But since they all know you're taken, it'll be…fine?" She uses her best coy smile on me and I concede, laughing at my friend.

Speaking of being taken, I shoot off a text to Palmer, letting him know the plan for the evening, hoping he doesn't already have something already laid out for us.

Me: Sterling is dragging me to a party back at the University tonight. That okay? She's currently assembling my entire wardrobe for the night. It's scary.

I drag a chair up to her mirror and begin applying my

makeup; blending, baking, contouring, brushing on shadows, and highlighting. My phone vibrates with a response.

Palmer: Sounds good, baby. You could use a night out. And you? Scary? Doubt it.

I smile to myself and snap a selfie with my lips puckered out, sending it back in a text. Setting my face and adding a splash of perfume, I take in my final look, nodding toward my reflection.

Not too shabby.

Sterling is dancing along to "Everyday" by Ariana Grande, and I can't help as the sway in my hips takes over and I join in, laughing harder than I have in a long time. I *did* need a girls' night. She pulls out a bottle of Jack and we take a few shots. The vibration on the desk signaling a new text pulls me from our impromptu dance party.

Palmer: Fuck. Annnnd I'm hard at work. Keep that top…I wanna peel it off with my teeth later.

I bite my lip to stifle the groan that threatens to escape my lips while reading his words.

Me: Sounds like a plan. Don't miss me too much…I'll call you later and we can take care of your…

I end the text with an eggplant and winking emoji and put my phone in my back pocket. Turning to Sterling, she claps her hands once.

"Let's have some damn *fun*, baby!" For the millionth time tonight, I shake my head and laugh along with my best friend as we head out front to catch our Uber.

It might be summer, but walking into the house party off campus, déjà vu hits me smack in the face, as well as the aroma of cannabis being passed around. I wave off the smog in front of me, following Sterling through the house into the kitchen. I say my hellos and hug a few people I haven't seen since classes ended just a few months ago.

How has it only been a few months? So much has happened, it seems like a year has passed.

I'm mid-catch-up with a girl who was in my poli-sci class from last semester when Sterling pulls me away.

"You need to play wing-woman. Hot guy from the café is here!" She nearly squeals, dragging me down the hallway and into the living room. I toss a wave over my shoulder, shrugging my apology to the girl whose name I can't remember. We make our way into the living room, and I see a small semi-circle is splayed around the furniture. Dead center is Sterling's crush. Jared? Jason? Jarret? I can't remember. She only ever calls him the guy from the café. As we saddle up on the ottoman together, across the coffee table from her crush, café boy, he suggests we all play Never Have I Ever. I groan and Sterling shoots daggers my way.

Oops, was that out loud?

I despise drinking games, but to appease Sterling and her obsession with this guy, I agree to play along. A familiar voice raises the hairs on the back of my neck and I turn to my left to find Spencer glowering at me while talking to one of his buddies. His eyes rake down my body, stopping on my very exposed cleavage to give me a wolfish grin before sipping his beer.

Shit. This was a bad idea…

"All right, you fuckers, if you're playing, get in here!" some random dude yells over the music. "LOCO" by Machine Gun Kelly booms through the surround sound in the place, muffling some of the side chatter.

"I'll start. Never have I ever…been arrested!" A tall guy with a beanie chimes in first, waiting for others to start drinking. People who have been arrested before take a swig, while hooting and hollering ensue.

Another guy I've never met adds a second choice. "Never have I ever kissed someone of the same sex!" Eyes scan the group playing, maybe twenty of us or so, waiting to see who takes a sip. I lift my Stella to my lips.

"Prove it!" A third guy I've never met yells toward Sterling and me, each finishing our swigs of beer. We both roll our eyes.

Resist the urge to gag at the predictability of the male species, Ken.

"Never have I ever shoplifted!" Another sip.

"Never have I ever…done acid!" Fewer people sip on this turn than the previous. Next is Sterling's turn.

"Never have I ever said the wrong name during sex!" she squeals, taking a sip of her beer.

"That's not how you play, Sterling," the girl to her right chimes in, tossing her hair over her shoulder, clearly annoyed with her. "You only drink if you *have* done the thing you claim you *never have I ever.*"

Sterling only shrugs in response, and I laugh, shaking my head at her faux pas.

"Never have I ever *fucked* an older man to make myself feel validated." *Spencer.* My lungs constrict and the chatter and laughter within the room goes silent.

His ice-cold stare meets mine from across the small living room, and I feel my lip curling into a snarl. I chug down the rest of my beer and stand, slamming the empty bottle down onto the coffee table. Our eyes stay locked and his vile laughter sears my already frayed nerves. I turn to leave the room.

I knew this was a bad idea.

"Oh, come on, Kennedy, baby, I was only just getting started!" He cackles, his voice seemingly closer than before. When I turn around to give my rebuttal, I find him standing no more than two feet from me.

"What is your fucking problem, Spencer? Can't handle the rejection? Save yourself the embarrassment and quit while you're ahead."

"Rejection?" He laughs out the word. "I don't know what world you're living in, sweetheart. I can have any bitch in this room tonight." He splays open his arms, spinning around slowly, taking in all the people watching our altercation.

"Any bitch but me, and that's what this is really about, isn't it?" I scoff, about ready to turn and leave Sterling at this party by herself and get home to Palmer. "Glad to see your face finally healed up, Spence. That was one hell of a shiner you had there." I smirk as I turn away.

His laughter stops abruptly as he latches onto me, swinging me back around to face him. His body is pressed flush against mine, and his large hands secure the tops of my arms, holding me tight in place.

"I wouldn't touch you with a ten-foot fucking pole after letting that scumbag, Colson, between your legs. Who knows what kind of shit he caught being someone's butt buddy in the penitentiary." An overwhelming smell of whiskey washes over me as Spencer's face inches closer to mine with each hate-filled word. "Flash those perfect tits around all you want—you're damaged goods, Darling." His words ricochet and the few people within earshot of us gasp at his vehemence.

The spiteful words about me mean little to nothing, but his talk of Palmer makes my blood boil, which is why I can't contain the words as they fall from my lips. I need to stop talking, I need to let this go; but I can't.

"Maybe so, Spence, but at least I've never had to fake it with *him*." The moment the last word escapes my mouth, I know it was a mistake. I see Spencer's airborne hand flying toward me before I can move out of its trajectory. The force of his slap knocks me over. The sting from his hand making contact with my face is nothing compared to the shooting pain emanating from just above my eyebrow as my face connects with the coffee table. Warm liquid coats the right side of my face. The room feels like it's spinning as I reach up to wipe the wetness off my brow.

Did someone spill their drink?

When I pull back, the first thing I see is my hand coated in a thick, red substance. My vision begins to blur and I hear someone calling my name.

Why do they sound so far away?

The last thing I see?

Blackness.

PALMER

THE FIRST THING I SEE is red.

I am going to fucking kill Spencer Laurent.

Kennedy is being attended to; the laceration above her brow bone requiring sutures. I ended up throwing my flannel over her tiny frame—the young Doctor-Ken-Doll look alike tending to her wound doesn't need to be ogling her tits. He opted to use Steri-Strips since the cut wasn't as large as all the blood would lead one to believe. It would also minimize the scarring.

Scarring.

My beautiful, perfect girl is going to be permanently scarred because of that fucking prick.

Have I mentioned that I am going to fucking kill Spencer Laurent?

I clasp her tiny hand in mine as Dr. Ken goes over after-care instructions with us, and I assure him that she will be taking it easy over the next few weeks. She may be suffering from a mild concussion, so he advised that I stay with her for the remainder of the night.

Planned on it, buddy.

I thank the doctor, assuring him that I will be with her every second. I press a kiss to my girl's temple opposite her new battle scar. Her tear-stained cheeks wretch my insides and I have to fight to keep my temper at bay, if only for her sake.

"Let's go, baby." I help ease her off the examination table.

"We'll stock up on junk food and play some board games or something—anything without a screen." She smiles timidly up at me, and I take her small hand in mine again as we exit the emergency room.

The only play-by-play of the evening I got from Sterling, who has since gone home. She was sobbing incoherently while explaining, blaming herself for what happened, for dragging her to that party. She was difficult to understand through her sniffling and wailing, so I only caught every few words. I zoned out once I heard that Spencer was there and that he put his fucking hands on her, but I think I got the gist of it. I'm hoping once we get settled in, Kennedy will be able to give me a better idea of what actually went down.

The one thing I do know for certain is that Spencer was hauled off in cuffs—and the irony is not lost on me. That's exactly where creep junior belongs—behind bars.

I open the passenger side door of my truck and help Kennedy hop inside, closing the door gently behind her. When I sidle up next to her from my side, she looks over at me with fresh tears coating her lashes.

"You don't need to be so gentle with me, Palmer. It's just a scratch." Her small self-deprecating smile destroys me, and I lean over to palm her cheek.

With a quick peck to her nose, I then press our foreheads together. "Just focusing on taking care of you so I don't wind up tracking him down, baby."

Our eyes lock once I pull away, and hers zone in on my mouth. Leaning forward, she devours my lips, her hungry mouth consuming mine, biting, teasing, her tongue exploring in a tantric dance-off. I ease away, both of us panting, and level her with a concerned look.

"Take it easy, Ken, we have plenty of time for all that." I

stroke back the tendril of matted down, bloody hair that fell just over her eyes. "I wanna make sure you're okay. Pacify me, if nothing else, okay? Please."

She nods and scoots into the center seat, buckling up. She leans her head against my shoulder and I start the truck, making my way toward her apartment.

CHAPTER TWENTY-EIGHT

PALMER

I SIP ON A BLACK coffee, my eyes darting back and forth between my nephew and my girlfriend, the two of them chatting away on this already stifling summer morning.

My girlfriend.

The word sounds almost juvenile and holds no bearings on how I truly feel about Kennedy, but I love using the title just the same. It makes what we have seem more real, giving it a name. My entire life I have never felt the way I feel about Kennedy—about anyone. I've gone through the motions; hookups, casual dating, a marriage from hell, and a few one-night stands in between. Nothing compares to what we have. I exhale as the consuming thoughts of how deeply embedded in my life she is rattle around my brain and I smile to myself. The thoughts drown out Travis going on about some concert he just went to, an artist I've never heard of but Kennedy knows.

Figures.

Lenny Kravitz's airy tune, serenading us about falling in love again, drifts through the coffee shop and I tap my fingers against my cardboard cup, enjoying the banter back and forth between two of my favorite people, loving that they have become close. My eyes linger on the laceration above Kennedy's sculpted brow, marring her porcelain smooth skin. I tense, remembering the events from the other night.

I should have been there.

The thought has plagued my mind since I found out. Spencer never would have been able to lay a hand on her had I been there. Shaking the hindsight thoughts from my head, I absentmindedly reach beside me and rub my thumb along the smooth skin of her forearm. She smiles back at me and I swear my heart sings.

Peet's Coffee Haüs is crowded today, the citizens of Beacon Hill clamber in and out to get their morning caffeine boost. By now, word of our relationship had spread throughout the town like wildfire, fizzling out to make way for the next round of juicy gossip. No one bats an eye at Kennedy and me together any longer. It feels so normal sitting here, enjoying the company of my girl so casually, as if nothing could possibly ruin our solitude today.

"It was absolutely *insane*, dude. I wish you could have come with me. I still say you work way too much." Travis whines to Kennedy, earning an eye roll and snicker in response.

"The only Kane Brown song worth listening to is 'What Ifs' and I have that one on my phone. Which means it's portable. Which means I saved myself an eighty-dollar concert ticket and a headache the next day." She shrugs, turning and giving me a closed-lip smile, scrunching up her nose.

"Lame. You are both so *lame*." Travis flings his head back and groans. "Uncle Cole, you're rubbing your old man ways off on her and it's really inconveniencing me." He looks back up to meet my eyes and I down the last of my coffee before answering.

"If we're being honest here, she couldn't attend since something else was rubbing off on her." I toss a devilish smile back and Kennedy snorts, whipping my shoulder with the back of her hand. The second the words register to Trav, the most revolted look spreads across his face, and his hands fly up to cover his ears.

"Jesus! Seriously? I could have lived my whole life without hearing that!" He slowly removes his hands, looking to Kennedy for backup, but she only offers a curt shrug in return. "You two are disgusting. Warn me before you say that kind of shit next time."

The three of us banter back and forth for the next twenty minutes while they finish their drinks. We're about to head out when Kennedy's carefree expression morphs into utter shock, and she stays plastered to her seat. I look over my shoulder, following where her gaze lands across the packed room, to a woman with mousy brown hair tied up in a neat bun. The woman looks poised, an olive-green jumpsuit accentuating her small frame. She almost looks…*familiar*? Though I can't quite place her.

The mystery woman begins making her way toward us, her brown eyes zeroed in on Kennedy, while an expression of contempt maims her otherwise attractive features. I look back at Kennedy as the woman power walks toward us, the same terrified expression still riddled on her face. Her normally tan complexion is ashen and the vice grip she has on the edge of our table has her knuckles bleached.

"Mom?" she quietly exclaims.

Oh, hell.

CHAPTER TWENTY-NINE

Kennedy

MY MOTHER APPROACHES OUR TABLE and instinctually, I stand up, clasping my hands in front of me, all but waiting for her assessment of what I'm wearing.

Old habits die hard.

Growing up, even though the money was never *ours* we still had to look the part of being wealthy. My mother would dress me to the nines—bows, dresses, and cute booties when I was younger, to more age appropriate sheath dresses and heels throughout my teen years. It wasn't until I left for college that I began dressing how I truly wanted. With my mother standing in front of me for the first time in years, my first instinct is to hide what I'm wearing. No doubt, my casual ripped up whitewash jeans, flip-flops, and black camisole showing off my tattoos are giving her a mini-stroke.

"Kennedy. How lovely to see you, you look…*comfortable.*" The last word escaping my mother's lips is uttered like a curse word. Her eye practically twitches with the forced attempt at a compliment. I inwardly cringe.

"Uh, hey." I clear my throat of the tension residing there.

"Hi, Mom. What are you doing here? I thought you weren't planning on getting to New York until next week?"

"Slight change of plans," she quips, suspiciously eyeing Travis and Palmer to either side of me. "Aren't you going to introduce me to your friends?" The venom in her tone assures me she's not in the best of moods today.

"Um, y-yes. Yes, this is Cole Palmer, and his nephew Travis Palmer." I motion to each of the men, both still seated while I'm stuck standing in place.

"Ah, yes, *Palmer*. You mentioned this on the phone." She extends her perfectly manicured hand out to shake Travis'. "You must be the boyfriend, I presume?"

Travis slowly shakes his head, looking at me for what to say, a worried expression beginning to form.

Oh, this should be fun...

"No, actually, *Cole* Palmer is my...boyfriend." I look down at my feet, ashamed that she can make those words feel so taboo. Rebecca Darling has that effect on most things in my life. Being the saint that he is, while hopefully not reading into my non-enthusiastic introduction, Palmer stands and extends his hand toward the ice queen herself.

"Pleasure to finally meet you, Rebecca. I've heard a lot about you." If I wasn't so utterly stunned by seeing my mother here, I might have snorted in response to Palmer's word choices. He *has* heard a lot about her, although none of it is good. I know the pleasure he speaks of is actually repugnance. Much like the malevolent woman she is, my mother looks at Palmer's outstretched hand like a bug she wants to squash, and then slowly her gaze moves to his face, disdain clear as day among her poised features.

"I see," she replies.

Realizing that she won't be shaking his hand anytime

soon, Palmer gives a quick once-over at his outstretched palm before running it through his hair. I shuffle closer to him, rubbing my hand along his lower back, my version of an apology at her cold dismissal. My mother takes notice of my gesture and scoffs.

"Oh, Kennedy. What are you doing?" She bows her head, snickering to herself. "You had it made with that Laurent boy—your future was set before you came here to stay with Jim." Her cold eyes meet mine as she raises her head and levels me with a pitiless stare. "Now look at you, reduced to some…some *sex doll* for a man nearly at his midlife crisis." She ridicules, causing Palmer to step forward.

"No disrespect, ma'am, but you are completely out of fucking line." His deep voice rumbles between the four of us. "Kennedy is so much more tha—"

"Oh, just lovely, the man of the hour jumping in to rescue her from her horrific mother! How quaint." Her eyes throw flames in Palmer's direction, and the passersby in Peet's are starting to take notice of the tension.

Somehow, the fog that seems to have rolled in with my mother lifts, and I step forward, beyond irritated with her barging into town and causing a scene. I stand between Palmer and my mother.

"Okay, just stop." I wave her off flippantly with my hand. "You're being ridiculous, Mother. I'm twenty-two years old, for God's sake! I can be with whoever *I* choose—not you. I love him and he loves me. I'm not sorry if that ruins your plans for my future. I've never been happier."

Palmer's hand gently squeezes my shoulder and I revel under his touch. My mother's eyes dart between Palmer, his hand against my skin, and me. Her mouth opens and closes, at a loss for what to say back. There are only a handful of times in my life where I've seen Rebecca Darling speechless. Today is one of those times. Finally, she erects her posture and her face goes rigid.

"What did you say? Surely I must have misheard you."

"No, you heard me. I said I love him. He loves me too."

The roar of laughter that erupts unrestrained from her throat causes me to jump.

"You are delusional, Kennedy. Completely delusional." She daintily wipes at the corners of her eyes where her laughter sprouted tears. "You must have lost your mind at the same time you received that gash on your head—I mean honestly, it looks dreadful."

"Does it? Because this *dreadful* gash was given to me by that precious *Laurent boy*." My attempt at keeping my anger and raised tone at bay fails miserably. "He is a poor excuse for a man, let alone a human being." I inch closer to her. "I moved here to escape *you* and if you can't accept my new life here, then that's fine, but you better stay the *fuck* away from me." My chest is heaving by the time the words fall from my mouth. All eyes in the room are on me and my little outburst, but I don't care. For once, I let my bottled emotions out and it feels damn good.

My mother stands stunned, for the second time today, and openly gapes at me. I collect my purse and take a hold of Palmer's hand, signaling for Travis to stand and leave with us. He hadn't moved a muscle since the moment she strode toward our table. I breeze past my mother and the curious glances surrounding us, out the door, and straight to the truck. I break contact with the warmth of Palmer's hand just long enough to enter the front seat, slamming the door with all my might behind me. Travis hops in the back at the same time Palmer slides into the driver's seat.

"Who needs coffee to wake you up first thing?" Travis chimes in from the backseat. "All a person needs is that bitch screaming at you to—"

Palmer turns and levels him with a glare. If I wasn't shaking like a leaf from the adrenaline coursing through my veins, I might have laughed.

Instead, I break down. My shoulders slump forward and my tears fall viciously with a loud cry erupting from my chest. My sobs are all I can hear resounding in my ears as Palmer pulls me to him, cradling my weeping body in his arms. His soft coos and terms of endearment spoken against my hair soothe me in ways I don't expect.

We stay just like this in the parking lot outside Peet's until my body is too wrecked to cry any longer.

CHAPTER THIRTY

PALMER

ALTHOUGH STILL SLIGHTLY VISIBLE, THE now pink gash on Kennedy's unblemished face has begun fading expeditiously. I run my fingers through her silky tresses strewn about my lap while her nose is buried deep within a book that she's almost finished.

We've kept a low profile now that her mother is in town—although I definitely will not hold my tongue should we have another run-in with the She-Devil—but cooping ourselves up on a Sunday in fear that she may see us seems ridiculous.

"Let's go somewhere today. I have an idea."

Her hazel irises look up, seeking mine, her sleepy gaze hiding her piqued curiosity well.

"Where to?"

"Nowhere crazy, just an idea I had the other night. I think today is a good day for it. It's fuckin' beautiful out anyway and you need some fresh air. Aids in the healing process."

"Oh yeah? Says who?" She snickers, her head still in my lap.

"Just this little thing called the world wide web. Which obviously means it's gotta be true."

I wiggle my eyebrows at her and lightly buck my hips as she sits upward, swinging her legs off the couch. I watch, enraptured, as she raises her arms in the air mid-stretch, only wearing one of my T-shirts and her panties. I stifle a groan and force myself to look away before I take her right here on my couch and we spend yet another day inside.

"Put on something slightly less comfortable and meet me in the truck in five. I'm timing you."

Kennedy stands just as my fingertips graze the slope of her ass cheek, erupting a squeal from her. She takes off, galloping up the stairs to change as I chuckle to myself.

No more than two minutes later, before I'm even ready to head out, Kennedy descends the stairs, tying her hair up in a messy bun, wearing cutoff shorts and band tee tied around her waist. Her eyes are free from their normal dark smoky look, and she looks even younger than she is, her bare face displaying her youth. I stand there, admiring and soaking her in like a rare sunset view.

"What?" Her eyes drop down her body, second-guessing her outfit. "Should I change?"

"No, definitely not. You look hot. Sometimes I just like to look at you."

The corners of her mouth lift, showcasing that heart attack inducing smile of hers.

"See? That right there. Fucking stunning." I raise her chin with the back of my thumb. "Did you ever have braces? Your teeth are every orthodontist's wet dream."

Kennedy tosses her head back, her breathy laughter echoing off my walls.

"I didn't, actually." She catches the tip of my thumb

between her perfectly straight teeth and bites down ever so gently. "Just lucky, I guess."

The seemingly innocent gesture gets my blood pumping to the nether regions of my body and I pluck my finger from her clenches, turning to situate myself more—comfortably—in my jeans. Her giggle behind me tells me she knows exactly what she does to me, and she loves every second of it.

"Come on, trouble. At least let me get through *part* of my plan before you tarnish my sainthood with your dirty ways."

Her signature eye roll makes its presense known.

Parking in the back lot of the shopping plaza downtown, there's no way for Kennedy to know where we're going. Getting bagels? New tattoo? In need of a new vacuum? Fancy some tea?

I clasp her hand in mine and lead her around the truck to our destination: Beacon Hill Books. Her eyes light up like a city skyline and she turns to me, that killer smile back upon her face.

Still so easy to please, Darling.

"What are we doing here?"

"Well, as the name of the store suggests, I believe we're here to get some books."

She swats my arm, a trend in our relationship, and lets out a laugh.

"I thought it might be fun to pick out a book for each other."

Through our conversations, I've learned that although you cannot drag her away from the horror realm in most everything else, she is a hopeless romantic when it comes to works of fiction and loves all those cheesy romance novels. We discussed literature, both new and old, over dinner the other night. She learned of my love for Stephen King, and I was shocked to learn, for as avid a reader as she is, she hadn't read a single one of his books. I was about to rectify that.

"I don't have any more room for books, though." She pouts next to me, still gazing longingly through the glass of the storefront. "You've seen my apartment. I'm gonna have to start using them as furniture at this rate."

As I look down at her, I brace myself for what I'm about to say.

"Have you ever thought of maybe, I don't know, keeping some at my place?"

Her round eyes search mine for a hidden meaning behind the question. I'm not one to mince words, and Kennedy knows this.

A coy smile begins to spread across her cheeks. "Are you asking my books to move in with you?"

"Just the books, yep. I'm giving them a drawer in the bedroom and a spare toothbrush too. Domestic shit and all that." I lightly press my knuckles to her cheek, and she giggles, grabbing ahold of my hand and clasping it between hers.

"What exactly are you asking me, Palmer?"

I rub her knuckles with my thumb and drop my head to close some of the distance between us.

"You, moving some of your stuff into my place. Maybe not all at once. I don't want you to feel like you can't have your own space...so maybe start small. Leave some clothes at my house so you don't always have to pack a bag when you come over. We'll get you a dresser, a spare charger, some toiletries, and if you want, whenever you're comfortable, maybe we make it…permanent?"

Her eyes widen farther and my heart begins a cadence within the walls of my chest.

Shit. Too soon. You just scared the ever-loving piss out of her, jackass. She only just moved into her own apartment and now you want her to move into your house? Smooth. Real smooth.

"I don't know…I mean…"

Fuck, this is about to get awkward.

"My boyfriend probably wouldn't appreciate me living with another man."

I noticeably relax.

"He's pretty scary around these parts. I would hate for him to find out and come pummel your ass." Our smiles mirror one another and I laugh, pressing my lips to hers.

"Just say yes like a normal person, Darling, you're giving me a coronary over here. I'll kick said boyfriend's ass while I'm banging his girl." I flick my tongue against her upper lip and she swings her arms over my shoulders, pulling herself up higher.

"Sounds like the makings of a kinky three-way, so I'm all for it." Her expression turns serious for just a moment, and she searches my eyes with her own. "I'm also all for your plan. We'll start small, and if you still like me after that, I say we make it permanent."

"Like you? *Meh.* Love you? Absolutely."

Our PDA resumes in front of the store before I break contact, leading her mouthwatering ass inside. "All right, since that's settled…divide and conquer. We each find one book of our taste that we want the other to read. Ready, set—" Before I can even finish, Kennedy sprints off, acquiring aggravated looks from the elderly crowd seated in the front lounge of the store. I shake my head, sniggering to myself.

Such a menace, this girl.

Kennedy

I'M PERUSING THE SHELVES, HUMMING along to "Lovers" by Anna of the North, already knowing just the book I'm choosing for Palmer. His idea to swap picks was so clever and thoughtful. Today is simply another reminder of how good he is to me. How *different* he is from anyone I've ever known. Spencer, and quite honestly anyone I've ever been with before, mocked me always reading.

It's just a waste of time.

It's so boring.

Palmer, while not quite the avid reader I am, at least appreciates this about me. The feeling of immersing yourself in another world, even if only for a little while, is like nothing else. Movies and music, while still wonderful, don't transport me to another place quite like a good book does. I've lived a thousand lives within the pages of my paperbacks—each one different than the last.

While scouring the shelves, a tall, dark figure to my left catches my attention and the hair on the back of my neck prickles. An older gentleman, maybe mid-forties, with salt and pepper hair that once was probably a dark, dirty blond in his earlier years, is staring straight at me. His cobalt eyes are trained on mine now that I've turned in his direction. *Why does he look familiar?* An uneasy feeling washes over me like déjà vu, and I quickly glance back toward the bookshelf in front of me—still hunting for the title I need.

Ah, found it!

Footsteps approach and I warm, knowing Palmer must have picked his option for me already.

"Don't peek!" I hug the thick binding to my chest. "I want mine to be a surpri—" I gasp as I turn, the book tumbling to the floor. The figure who approached me isn't Palmer after all, but the snooping stranger from only a moment ago.

"Sorry, dear, didn't mean to startle you." The unknown man bends at the waist to pick up the book I dropped. As he hands it to me, his fingers linger a bit too long against mine for my liking, and I pull the book from his grip.

"Thank you." I turn to leave the romance and self-help section of the store, when Mr. Creepy latches onto my arm, turning me to face him yet again, applying just enough pressure to be uncomfortable.

"We have not yet had the pleasure of meeting each other, Ms. Darling. I've heard so much about you." His slightly crooked grin showcases abnormally white teeth, his canines much sharper than the average person's, giving him an unnatural, almost vampiric look. His nose has a bump in the center, almost as if it had been broken in the past. Aside from the chilling feeling he gives me, he's actually pretty handsome.

"I'm sorry." I pull my arm from his clutches. "Do I know you?" I begin to back away, creating some much-needed space between us. My back collides with the shelf, halting my departure, and he snickers, shaking his head.

"No, you don't know me, beautiful girl, but I know *plenty* about you." He winks, his perfectly shaped eyebrows rising and falling on his slightly wrinkled and tan forehead. His three-piece suit seems a bit much for the weather gracing us mid-August, but I guess fashion knows no seasonal bounds when you're a creepy bastard.

"Right." I nod, laughing uncomfortably as I search for an out. "Well, it was…*interesting* meeting you, but I gotta get going. Have a good one." I weave around the still anonymous man, and as I'm about to descend the stairs in search of my human solace, the man's cool voice rings out a chilling farewell.

"Goodbye, Kennedy. Tell Colson an old *friend* says hello."

I stop, my foot dangling above the top step, and turn to face the stranger over my shoulder.

"I'll be seeing you again soon, beautiful girl. You can count on it." His sneer causes goose bumps to scatter the whole length of my body and I bolt down the stairs.

PALMER

KENNEDY PLOPS HER CHOSEN BOOK for me down on the counter and the Mrs. Potts sounding cashier continues her ramblings about the deal the store has going on currently.

Not interested, lady.

I catch a peek at the bright red spine of the book Kennedy chose. *A Pound of Flesh* by Sophie Jackson. Sounds dirty. *I hope it's dirty.* I can't wait for her to start reading what I picked out for her. It isn't his most popular book, but it's a good one nonetheless. *Gerald's Game* is definitely not within her normal repertoire, but I think she'll still enjoy it.

Kennedy's petite frame is pressed tightly against me as

we wait. Her delicate fingers clutch onto my bicep tighter than usual, and she keeps looking around the store as if she's searching for something.

Or someone.

"Was there something else you wanted to get, baby? There's no rush." I peer down at her and she simply shakes her head while continuing to scour the first floor of the bookstore. Odd.

I pay for our books and then snatch Kennedy's hand while we exit the musty smelling store. Her normally playful demeanor is gone, replaced instead by one on edge and rigid. I'm suddenly worried. What the hell happened between our separation earlier and now?

"Everything go okay in there? You feeling all right?"

"What? Yeah—yes, I'm fine. Sorry." She still hasn't even looked my way since we left. Pulling out the big guns, I offer to take her to get Pinkberry across the street; if some ruby red grapefruit froyo doesn't snap her out of this—I got nothin'.

She politely declines.

Okay, what the fuck…

Stopping us in the middle of the sidewalk, I turn to face her, peering down at her angelic face.

"Seriously, babe…what is going on? You look like you've just seen a ghost, you're looking around like a paranoid schizo, *and* you turned down froyo. Something is up and you're freaking me out. *Spill.*"

Finally, her timid gaze meets mine, and I soften, cradling her head in my hands.

"Please? Maybe I can help."

I search her eyes, watching her throat convulse as she swallows, gulping down her, what? Fear? Apprehension? This can't be good.

"A man…" she starts.

A man? What?

"He stopped me in there. He was really creepy and looked familiar somehow. I don't know. He said he knows me, and you. He grabbed my arm when I went to leave…"

I will fucking kill…

"He said he's an old friend of yours."

The hair on my arms stands at attention, my senses on high alert. I can't think of who it may have been, especially claiming to be a friend of mine. I have a total of like three friends and Kennedy has met them all…

"He didn't give you a name? A last name? Nothing?"

How fucking weird.

"No. He had sort of graying hair, dark blue eyes, and he was wearing this, like, fancy suit. Which I thought was odd since it's summertime and—"

Kennedy's voice drones on in the background, my mind moving at one hundred miles per hour. *Fancy suit, gray hair, blue eyes…old friend.* It all makes sense. I haven't seen him for years—I was told he was off on some cross-country tour, buying up restaurants and spreading his filth along the mid-west. I hadn't planned for the day he returned to Beacon Hill. A cloud of red envelops me, my brain short-circuits, and I feel nauseous. He knows who Kennedy is and that's *bad*. Especially after recent events.

He is ruthless. He is unforgiving. He is above the law.

Jason Laurent is back in town.

CHAPTER THIRTY-ONE

PALMER

NOT ONLY ARE WE HIDING out from Kennedy's wretched mother, but now we also have fucking Jason Laurent to worry about. Doesn't sound too bad, until you consider the fact that Beacon Hill is about the size of a football field. We've been hunkered down at my place when neither of us is working, and that's worked out well for me, considering Kennedy's been my alarm clock for the past week—her mouth working me deep into her throat tends to do the trick better than my usual cup of coffee.

I've tried to have her stay here since our bookstore run-in. My overprotective nature when it comes to Kennedy Darling has been kicked into overdrive. My hackles are up and I'm ready to bare my teeth and pounce, ripping the jugular from anyone attempting to harm her, if need be. No one, and I do mean no one, will so much as breathe heavily in my girl's direction without hearing from me.

With the wedding being this evening, hiding out between my sheets, unfortunately, isn't on the menu. I have to parade around in a penguin suit, wishing pleasantries to the happy couple and making small talk with people I couldn't care less about.

We're currently at Kennedy's apartment and she's been getting ready for the past hour. I'm growing impatient.

"Babe! I've grown a full fucking beard since you started getting dressed!" I yell from my spot on her couch. "If I don't hear signs of life soon, I'm coming in, guns a-blazin'!" I hear muffled laughter behind her bedroom door and I smile to myself, loving that I can still keep her laughing.

"I'll be out in five, quit your bitching!"

I busy myself in the kitchen and grab a beer to occupy myself when I hear heels clacking against the hardwood. I turn to complain, something about withering away to nothing, when all thoughts drift from my head.

Holy. Fucking. Shit.

Kennedy is dressed to the damn nines tonight. Her long, flowing, silver tresses are curled in the way I love, but pinned all to one side, showcasing her slender neck. Her makeup is flawless—the girl is the next Picasso with that shit. Her dark brows are perfectly shaped, her hazel eyes highlighted by the sexy smokiness surrounding them and framed by her long lashes. Beautiful bronzed and glowing skin trails down the front of the dress where a deep V-cut showcases her perfectly supple breasts. And that dress? *Shit.* It's champagne-colored and long, skimming just above her ankles, flowing gently behind her. The sequins adorning the fabric catch the light, making her glow impeccably.

"Pick up your jaw, old man." Her smug smile brings me back to the present and I shake my head like a wet dog, causing her laughter to return. "You're insane."

"Insane for you, maybe." I close the distance between us and peck a kiss to her hairline. "Goddamn, you are fucking *gorgeous*, baby."

"Thank you." Her cheeks turn a flushed pink. "Are you meeting me there or riding with me?"

"I was going to meet you since you have to be there long before I have to be—chosen one in the wedding party and all."

She nods and turns, bending to snatch her purse off the entryway bench. The view of her perfectly sculpted ass before me causes my already hardening cock from seeing her all dressed up, to lurch in my pants.

I slide my hand up the small of her back, ascending the curve of her spine. Kennedy stands with her back to me and presses her ass into my groin. Her low purr tells me she's just as turned on by the situation down there as I am for sporting it. I catch a glimpse of her in the full-length mirror to the left of us, as her eyes flutter closed. Gliding my fingers along her exposed collarbone, I shift us just slightly so she can see us in the mirror as well. My trail leads me down the deep cut in the front, and I graze the exposed mound of her breast. Her eyes open, the fire blazing within them meeting mine as I stand behind her. She's practically panting.

"Have five minutes to spare?" I whisper, nipping at her ear and watch as cold shivers break out across her sun-kissed skin.

"I could spare a few. What do you have in mind?" She begins to turn, and I halt her, squaring her shoulders to our reflection.

"I want you to watch," I chide, my lips ever so gently nibbling down the side of her neck to her shoulder. "I'm very fond of this dress." I trail my hand down her ribcage, causing her body to shiver beneath my fingertips, to another long slit from the top of her thigh to the base of the fabric. "Especially this part right here. I think we can find plenty of uses for this tonight." I continue my exploration with my lips up and down her neck, her panting breaths growing more urgent.

"Touch me, please, Palmer. I'm so wet."

Jesus fucking Christ.

"Gather the loose fabric for me, baby." I assist her in bunching the sheer champagne textile around her waist. "And hold on tight." I sink my teeth into her neck, hard, and she whimpers.

Kennedy

MY EYES ARE GLUED IN place to his large, tattooed hands working their way down my body. Seeing him this way is so damn erotic, I could come from his perusal in the reflection alone. The hunger in his eyes for me is nearly my undoing. In contrast to the warmness in my panties, Palmer's fingers are cold as they breach the band of my thong and he dips his fingers lower. The contact of one large finger brushing against my sensitive flesh causes me to jump, and he chuckles against my neck.

"I thought I said hold tight," he purrs in my ear and good God, his voice is liquid sex. His magic fingers part my folds, working me into a frenzy, building me higher. "Fuck, you weren't kidding. You're soaked, baby."

I'm panting like a dog in heat as Palmer removes his fingers from between my legs and presses a wet digit between my lips, and I suck. My eyes flutter closed at the sensations all around me—the hardness pressing into my lower back, the heat emanating off his body, the wetness pooling between my thighs, the taste of me on Palmer's finger—it's too much. I moan, pressing harder against him as I suck him into my mouth deeper, twirling my tongue around his finger, lapping up every last bit of me on him.

"*Fuck…*yes, Ken, just like that. Do you want to come, baby?" Our eyes meet in the glass across from us and I simply nod. "Say it. Tell me."

"Yes."

His eyebrow raises in question, pressing me for more.

"I want to come. Please."

The wolfish grin that spreads along his face exposing his canines does me in and he removes his finger from my mouth with a loud *pop.*

He finds his target between my legs yet again, and he begins moving his fingers slowly inside of me, curling just so, hitting that magic ridge just inside my entrance. His kisses up and down my neck are exactly the right amount of sweetness compared to the ambush he's providing my core.

"Look how fucking stunning you are," he whispers against my skin, locking eyes with me in the mirror. I can see that my cheeks are flushed pink, and my chest is heaving. I wet my lips. My eyes burn wild with lust before me. My stomach tightens as he continues his merciless kneading. I begin to close my eyes, my orgasm building at the base of my spine, ready to snap through me at a moment's notice.

"No." He stills his movements. "Open your eyes." Our eyes connect once more. The heat blazing in his tells me everything I need to know about his feelings for me. This man loves me. There's no disputing that fact. He begins moving once again, and I roll my head back to rest against his shoulder, my heart warming along with the ball of fire in my belly that begins shooting off sparks in all directions—just waiting to engulf me completely from the inside out. Palmer's free hand flexes across my upper abdomen, rubbing circles into the exposed flesh with his thumb, coaxing the finale from me.

My legs start to shake, and it takes everything in me to stay upright.

"That's right, baby," Palmer growls his request into my flesh as he bites down. "Come for me, Kennedy. *Right now.*"

My vision blurs, the two of us in the mirror simply shapes as I detonate around him. I scream out his name and he grunts, pumping faster into me.

When my convulsions slow, he eases his fingers out, allowing me to drop the fabric. The material bunches at my feet and I turn slowly on wobbly legs, facing the man who just made me see stars in broad daylight.

I peck a kiss to his lips, careful not to smear my taupe lipstick.

"Well, that's a new favorite," I tease, and he gives me a boyish grin—my favorite one of all.

"That dress turned me into a caveman. I couldn't contain it."

"Oh, this *dress* turned you into a caveman?" I giggle. "What exactly are you normally, then?"

He slaps my ass playfully and scoots me toward the front door.

"A gentleman." He gives me one last kiss to the top of my head, leaning his forearm against the doorframe. "Have fun. I'll see you soon, beautiful. I'll be the one looking wildly out of place."

I make my way down my front steps, grinning, when I hear him calling to me again.

"And that was only four minutes! I owe you one later!"

I float the rest of the way to my car, with a smile large enough to split my face in two.

CHAPTER THIRTY-TWO

Kennedy

THE CEREMONY WENT OFF WITHOUT a hitch, and I haven't been able to wipe the smile from my face since I arrived. Jim and Melissa's vow exchange left not a dry eye in the area, save for, of course, my brooding mechanic, who stood in the back.

I converse with the other bridesmaids after the throwing of the bouquet, which thankfully I *didn't* catch. As much as people have accepted my relationship with Palmer, somehow I don't quite see the myth for potential wedding bells keeping the side chatter at bay.

The mingling voices around me blur into white noise once I soak in Palmer's figure standing across the way from me. My man can wear the hell out of a suit jacket. The charcoal gray fabric hugs his large frame in all the right ways and his few-days-old scruff offsets the formality of the suit, making him all the more handsome. His tatted knuckles peek out the bottom of his jacket, the juxtaposition nearly making my mouth water. I'm not the only one who appreciates the sight; nearly every female in the vicinity has their jaw on the floor openly gaping at Palmer.

And he's all mine. Eat your hearts out, ladies.

Standing toward the edge of the makeshift dance floor, his expression is hard to read as he stares back at me. Slowly, he begins to close the distance between us. The dancing has already begun, and he weaves his way through the jumping, shimmying, and grinding bodies on his quest over to me, ignoring the looks of appreciation on his trek. Stopping just a pace before me, he cups my cheek, the corners of his mouth lifting ever so slightly. Shaking his head, he closes his eyes, opening them only a second later.

"You are so fucking beautiful." My heart swells, beating erratically within my chest. "Every single person here can't keep their eyes off you, Ken." He kisses the tip of my nose, the sweetest gesture coming from this brute of a man.

"Thank you." I smile. "If I tell you that you look beautiful, too, are you going to make me pay for it later?"

The laugh that emanates from him rumbles through the crowd like thunder. Eyes turn toward us, scouring to find the source of the roaring sound. If Palmer takes notice, he doesn't show it, never once removing his eyes from mine.

"I might. But that's later. Right now, I just wanna capture how beautiful you look." He pulls out his phone and grabs me by the waist.

The utter disbelief on my face makes him pause, his arm outstretched before us, ready to snap a photo.

"What?" He peers down at me.

"I just—you don't strike me as the *let's take a selfie,* person." I chuckle, biting on my thumbnail.

"I'm not...normally," he admits, clearing his throat and turning his attention back to the front-facing camera. "But one won't hurt."

I lean into Palmer, my hand finding the curve of his pectoral resting above the steady drum of his heart. Our smiles mirror one another on the touch screen and my heart flutters. *Click.* Palmer snaps our picture, freezing this moment in time forever. I pull away, but his hand grips my hip tighter, keeping our bodies flush against one another.

"Just one more." His smirk is back. I love this playful side of him. The one only I'm privy to, which makes it all the more special to me. I inch up on my tiptoes to peck a kiss to his cheek. Out of the corner of my eye, I see him snap another. *Click.* I lower and turn to face the camera once again, scrunching my face and sticking out my tongue—he makes the same face. *Click.*

"Seriously, you look so handsome." I brush a finger across his stubbled cheek. "I'm not used to you so dressed up. It's nice." He only shrugs, his cheeks pinking slightly at the compliment. I can't help but smile to myself at his change in demeanor.

"I never thought I would see the day." Jim's voice, full of humor, pops the bubble of our own little world we're in. "Cole Palmer taking a selfie and wearing a suit, no less." He lightheartedly punches Palmer's arm, the two of them chuckling. "But with this beauty on your arm, even you don't look half bad."

I leave the warm embrace of Palmer's arms and make my way toward my uncle, throwing myself into his open arms. "I'm so happy for you," I whisper in his ear. As I pull away, I see a faint misting of tears forming on his bottom lashes, threatening to spill. Blinking them away quickly, he beams down at me.

"Thank you, Kenny girl. You look—" He holds me back at arm's length and shakes his head in disbelief. "You're absolutely stunning. I wish Colby could be here with us today, the three of us swapping insults and laughing at everything and nothing at the same time."

I tense within his grasp. I haven't spoken a word about my brother to Palmer. *Yet*. I've been meaning to. I just haven't wanted to burst our bubble that we've been in together for the past few months. Turning to gauge his expression and brace myself for the questions about to arise, I notice that he must not have heard. His warm smile directed toward Jim's and my exchange hasn't changed.

Sensing my discomfort, Jim places his arm around my shoulders and pulls me in, pressing a kiss to my temple.

"All right, enough sappy shit. Cole, take this beautiful girl out there and get dancing!" He wags his eyebrows at a glowering Palmer, clearly *not* thrilled by the idea. "I'll make sure to snap a few photos, seeing how you're so fond of those."

Jim scampers a few feet away before Palmer can have his say, and I shriek, dragging my handsome date through the writhing bodies onto the dance floor.

"And hands where I can see them!" Jim yells, his two fingers making the *I'm watching you* gesture just as "Timber" by Pitbull begins.

Palmer's groan of objection has me laughing hysterically. I begin twirling around him, his head swiveling while trying to keep me, no doubt a blur at this rate, within his sights. Eventually, he stops, launching his head back in laughter, and joins in. We're jumping, swaying, and laughing; our limbs tangled and waving as I sing along to all the Ke$ha parts. I haven't had this much fun in so long, and seeing the happiness within those green eyes of Palmer's, I know he feels the same.

The music fades out as the song ends, replaced by the high-pitched screech of a microphone.

"Guess this thing works, huh?" My uncle's voice rings out larger than life through the external speakers scattered throughout the white tent above us, causing a few chuckles to resound. "I just want to take a moment and thank you all for coming out and sharing our special day with us. Mel and I could not be surrounded by more supportive family and friends, and we appreciate you all tremendously." Jim clears his throat. "At this time, we ask that you all take a moment of reflection in memory of those who cannot be here with us today—Melissa's father, Jerry Lewis, and my nephew, Colby Darling." Jim makes a sympathetic grin in my direction and then bows his head. The room goes still as those around us take their moment of silence.

The thumping of my heart smashing against my rib cage is all I hear as the room begins to spin. My vision blurs with tears and I turn to look at Palmer. His confused expression is clear as day and I can't look away.

Just as I'm about to flee from under his scorching gaze still latched onto me, I hear the beginnings of a slow clap, followed by a menacing, and eerily familiar chuckle.

Mom?

I turn to face the corner of the tent that the chilling sound is coming from, and find her, champagne flute in hand, as the crowd begins to part around her like the Queen Bee she is. The back of my neck tingles from the imminent blow-up.

What the hell is she doing here?

"*Hilarious.* This whole thing is truly comical." She sips her drink, swaying as she makes her way to me. I see Jim walking briskly toward the both of us, coming from the opposite side of the makeshift wooden dance floor.

I can't move. I can't breathe. I can't think.

Rebecca Darling may not be good at much, never having had to actually work for anything a single day in her life, but causing a scene has always been one of her specialties. I smell the alcohol, mixed with her floral Chanel perfume wafting toward me, singeing the inside of my nostrils as she approaches.

"Rebecca, you need to leave. You weren't invited for this very reason." Jim's voice is much sterner than I have ever heard it before. My mother clucks her tongue in annoyance and sucks her teeth in distaste at the scene before her—my uncle dashing in to kick her out, and my *lover*, as she has so graciously put it, standing behind me ready to pounce.

"You invite murderers to your nuptials, but not your own sister? My, my, your manners need some work, dear brother."

The gasp that slips from between my lips lures her arctic glower in my direction.

"What? Haven't divulged that piece of information to your *man*, yet?" She swallows down the remaining contents of her drink, dropping the delicate glass to shatter on the floor at her feet. Her hatred for me shines through the glassy haze coating her eyes—she would take me down with her before ever admitting that she's the one in the wrong.

A strong hand at my lower back steels me against her scowl, and I straighten. Palmer makes his way to my side, leveling the woman who birthed me with a heated glare of his own.

"Let's take this elsewhere—this is not the time nor the place to stir shit up. Let's just—"

"Oh, *let's just* nothing!" Spit soars as she screams. "This does not concern *you*, you fucking cradle robber! You do not even know this girl and what she has done to me, to our family. *My* family!" Her heaving chest and words filled with hate have me shrinking within myself. The embarrassment she's causing me, Jim, *everyone*. I can't take it.

I storm past my mother, towing her arm along with mine. She trips over her too-tall heels, quickening her steps to keep pace with me. I drag her through the stunned audience forming around us and lead her outside the tent toward the edge of the lake—at least here we have *some* privacy. Jim, Palmer, and Travis follow us outside.

When I stop moving, her arm tugs free from my grasp, and she flattens the errant strands of hair that have escaped her topknot.

"She didn't tell you, did she?" she probes. "Her twin brother, Colby? Your precious little gem killed my baby boy with her selfishness!"

CHAPTER THIRTY-THREE

PALMER

NOW, I AM IN MY mid-thirties, and the music had been loud under the tent, but surely my hearing can't be *that* bad. I could have sworn she just said Kennedy...*killed*...her brother.

"What the hell are you spewing off about?" I step forward and she takes one back. Considering I have nearly two feet on the woman, I'm not surprised that she backs down. I've never once hit a woman, or even come close, but she doesn't know that.

"She's a drunk mess and she's doing what she always does, places blame where it doesn't belong, and I won't stand for it." Jim steps in from outside my peripheral. "Kennedy wasn't driving the car that night, Rebecca. She is not the villain here. There *are* no villains here."

I am so lost.

"All she had to do was pick me up!" Rebecca's shrieks.

"She is not the parent, Rebecca! Jesus, you're a mess. You have always been a mess. Stop blaming this on her before you lose the only child you have left! The loss of Colby was, and still is, indescribably painful—but this whole charade is getting ridiculous." Jim's voice is thunderous. No doubt everyone still underneath the tent can hear the exchange. I turn, muttering an order for Travis to run back and get them to start playing music again, hopefully, to drown out the heated confrontation unfolding.

"Oh, get off your damn high horse, Jim. I asked for a *ride*, which is the *responsible* thing to do, isn't it? My precious daughter couldn't be dragged away from her life for more than five minutes to help her own mother! That's what's ridiculous!"

I watch as Kennedy's mother begins pacing, her words tumbling out in a jumbled mess. Kennedy, normally oozing confidence and self-assurance, looks like a shell of her radiant self. Her shoulders are rounded forward and slouched, while her face is completely crumpled. A lone tear streams down her cheek. I make my way to her, listening to her mother spew off as I go. Taking her frail body in my arms, I cocoon her against my chest and smooth back her hair. I hear "We Are Family" begin playing faintly in the distance—*thank God for Travis and his sick sense of humor.*

"Your children are not responsible for parenting you, Rebecca, get that through your head! You have a problem. You are drunk every waking hour of the day! Colby *chose* to pick you up that night. No one could have known what was going to happen. If Kennedy had been the one to pick you up smashed from a day of binge drinking, *she* could likely be the one we're mourning now."

I shudder at the thought.

The next words out of Rebecca's mouth are so silent I question whether she said them at all.

"I wish she were."

Kennedy's small whimper beneath my chin is the only

proof that I'm not imagining the words. I clutch her closer to my chest, my heart breaking for this girl who turned my world upside down only months ago.

"Get the fuck out."

The vehemence in my voice causes both Jim and Rebecca to turn to me. Her eyes go wide as she takes in the view of her child in my arms.

"Now. I won't say it again." I reluctantly let go of Kennedy, taking small steps toward this heartless woman before me. "Leave. The fact that you showed up on your brother's *wedding* day to dig up past shit, reeking of booze and throwing insults is enough." I step closer, looking down my nose at the poor excuse of a woman before me. "I will not stand by and let you speak this way about her. I'll carry you kicking and screaming over my shoulder if I have to. But you *will not* cause one more moment of distress for her. I'll make damn sure of that."

Rebecca's jaw works under her skin, itching to get the next word in. With a shake of my head, I signal her to choose wisely. She sneers and lets out an exasperated huff. Turning on her expensive heel, she leaves the property with her tail between her legs. Jim follows, much to my chagrin. If it were me, I wouldn't waste my fucking energy on the bitch.

The sobs coming from behind me shatter the rest of the splintered organ within my chest.

I turn just as Kennedy falls into my arms. Her tears begin soaking through the front of my dress shirt. Her fragile body quakes between my arms and I squeeze onto her so tight, just hoping I can hold her together this way. I'm nearly positive she won't be able to breathe soon if I don't let up.

"Do you want to go home, baby?" I whisper against her hair.

Her sobs slow to small snivels, and like a frail bird in my

grasp, one who just collided with a vehicle, she shakes. My heart cracks in half for my grieving girl.

"No. I just need to clean myself up. I don't want to leave Jim and Melissa on their wedding day just because of her." She straightens her spine, looking up at me, her eyes pooling with more tears. "I'm so sorry I didn't tell you about Colby. I—"

"Have nothing to apologize for." I cut her off. "*Nothing*. Do you hear me?"

Using my thumbs, I brush aside the tears streaming down her gorgeous face. This girl is too perfect for words. She just had to stand by, listening to her mother spew off the most hurtful words, and here she is, worried about not wanting to ruin someone *else's* day. The love I have for her only grows in that moment, and I'm helpless against it. My heart, body, and soul forever tied to the woman before me.

"I love you." Melding my lips with hers, she hums into my mouth, deepening our embrace.

"Say it again," she whispers, and I let myself smile.

"I love you."

"Again," she chokes. The salty wetness from new tears works its way into our kiss, and I pull away to peer down at her. Kennedy's eyes are scrunched tight, pain etched into her delicate features. I can tell, by her face alone, that all she needs is to hear these three words repeatedly. I want nothing more than to take away the pain and if this is all she needs to hear for now, I'll say it as many times, and as often as she needs to hear it. Taking her angelic face between my fingers, I angle her head upward so I can stare into her copper and emerald eyes.

"I love you. So goddamn much."

She nods in my grasp, her bottom lip trembling.

"I love you, too."

I place a quick kiss to her lips and help hide the evidence of her tears before we stroll back under the tent. I hand her the Corona I had been sipping on and she takes it, gulping down the remaining liquid.

The rest of the night, Kennedy spends dancing, drinking, and laughing—with me keeping a watchful eye on her—worried her sudden carefree demeanor is merely a Band-Aid for the flood about to erupt once the night is over and the remnants of her mother's cruel words fully sink in.

The rumble of the highway beneath my tires lulls Kennedy's inebriated body to sleep. Her soft snores blend into Puddle of Mud's "Blurry," the soft rock ballad mixing well with the sounds. I've already pulled off at a rest stop and grabbed a water and some Advil—she'll need both when she wakes up.

This girl can toss them back. *Holy shit.* I've never seen her drink quite this much before—she took the open bar for the bridal party suggestion as gospel, drinking her weight in liquor throughout the night. Numbing the pain with alcohol, while normally I would advise against it, was decidedly necessary tonight. Hearing your own mother say she wishes you were the one to die in a fatal car crash over your own sibling has to be a colossal pill to swallow. The liquor, in this case, was merely lubricating the pill's descent. I watched over her and made sure she was safe, even danced when she requested my presence—something I never do unless I'm at *Elixir* or heavily intoxicated.

Allowing myself a glance, I take in her tiny frame swallowed up by my jacket draped around her shoulders. I realize fully that I would do just about anything to shield her from pain. To make her happy. To stand before her and take every bit of bad in the world for myself just to spare her even an ounce of hurt. She is everything to me. Everything I never knew I needed.

Tonight, I plan to take her to my place and hold her tight while she lets her chainsaw like snores rip in my ears—and I'll love every goddamn moment of it.

"Do you hate me?"

Kennedy's small voice croaks from the passenger seat. Her body had shifted while she was asleep, and is now facing me with her eyes trained to the side of my skull. I can feel them like lasers, searing holes into my flesh.

Turning the music down to a low buzz, I glance her way briefly, making eye contact with her. Her silver curls are in disarray and her dress is disheveled from curling her legs up under her, making her already small fame significantly smaller, much like a child's.

"I don't think I could ever hate you," I tell her. And I mean it. "I just wish you had told me about him. That's a *huge* part of your life. I mean, I understand why you didn't, but it doesn't change the fact that I wish you had let me in. That's...a lot to deal with on your own." I begin drawing circles on her exposed kneecap with my thumb, lulling her eyes closed.

She nods, wiping the black smudges from under her eyes,

only succeeding in making them worse. "I haven't talked to anyone about it. I don't know how."

"Why not just start at the beginning?"

Kennedy

"I ALWAYS KNEW MY LIFE would be...*different* from what she wanted it to be." I shrug, staring at the lit-up dashboard, the blue neon lights a welcome distraction. "I was always content sitting in my room reading and being by myself. My twin brother, Colby, was the exact opposite. He was this hotshot football player—a different girl every week kind of lifestyle—but he was *good*, you know? He would never walk all over people to get what he wanted. He just got it. He worked hard and he played harder. We were so similar, but yet so different at the same time. He was the other half of me. Colby Darling was the golden child and I was the mistake, the extra baby she never asked for but got anyway."

Clearing his throat, Palmer let out the words, no doubt at the tip of his tongue. "What happened that night?"

"Our mother, as usual, was in town and three sheets to the wind by two in the afternoon and kept up her day drinking long into the night. I was out that night, on a date actually, when she called me asking for a ride. I told her no, that I wasn't going to keep picking up after her and carting her around from one place to another whenever she needed me. It never occurred to me that she might call Colby—she never asked him for anything. It was always just me. My mother has always disliked me, or maybe resented me. I was never going to make her the money she so badly craved like Colby would with his big-time sports dreams. He was another meal ticket to her, while she wrote me off long ago. Actually, thinking back on it now, I think that night was the first time I ever actually said no to her." I chuckle under my breath, the effects of the alcohol still coursing through my veins. My head beginning to smart with the early stages of a headache.

Tomorrow is going to be rough.

"She called Colby, *knowing* he hadn't been sleeping well. He was working himself to the bone trying to keep up with his football scholarship. He had been popping Adderall like Tic Tacs for the last few months and was in dire need of some actual sleep. He was probably just as impaired driving that night as my mother would have been."

Palmer shifts his grip on the steering wheel and looks at me once, fleetingly.

"I guess I don't understand where she gets the *murderer* charade from. You weren't even there that night."

I peer past Palmer's arm gripping the wheel, and out the driver's side window, watching the trees zip past us.

"I didn't need to be. In her eyes, he was just her last resort after I denied her. She wholeheartedly believes it's my fault—she needed somewhere to place the blame, wrong or right, and she found it. If I had been the one driving, who knows, maybe the accident never would have happened. I think about that the most. The what-ifs. What I could have done differently that day from the moment I woke up until I got the call that night. Some days even I blame myself too."

Those what-ifs eat me alive. Those what-ifs keep me up some nights, each different scenario playing out. I have thought out hundreds of different outcomes of that night, and each time I do something different, each time he is still here—*with me.*

"That's shit—I'm sorry, but that's complete and utter shit. You did *nothing* wrong, Kennedy. She's the parent, and from what I've seen and heard, not the best one. Her poor judgment does not just become your fault when it's convenient, or easier to place the blame elsewhere. *Bullshit.*"

We've stopped moving, and I'm not sure when that happened. Seated in the truck in Palmer's driveway, my limbs feel heavy, even as the weight of talking about that night somewhat has lifted from my chest. I feel…unsettled somehow.

"Do you mind just taking me back to my apartment?" I brave a glance in his direction, bracing myself for his reaction to my request.

"Um, sure…yeah, we can go to your place."

We.

The short ride to my apartment is quiet, save for the hum of the stereo, Default's raspy chorus filling the silence, somehow calming the churning in my stomach. As we slow to a stop, I quickly grab my purse and exit his truck. I hear the cut of the engine and Palmer's footsteps thumping heavily behind me, as we both ascend my front steps in cadence. When I reach the top landing, I turn, and his body crashes into mine, nearly toppling me over. He halts, backing down a step to take in my neutral expression.

"I'm just gonna go to bed."

I know I'm pushing him away, giving him the cold shoulder when he's done nothing, but I can't stop.

My own mother doesn't want me…why should he?

"Okay, that's fine. I could sleep." He starts to move again, but I stay rooted in place. My eyes are glued to his feet. I can't bear to look him in the eyes.

"I meant…alone." I feel too exposed, as if my flesh is one giant, gaping wound and the entire world can see in, dissecting my thoughts. The one thing I'm good at, the only thing I know how to do when I feel this exposed is to run— and I will.

"Kennedy." His deep voice sends pleasure waves straight to my groin. I ignore them, slowly peering up at him from under my lashes.

"What?"

"What the hell are you doing?"

"I just…"

"No." The authoritarian tone of his voice makes me feel small, like a child. "Don't tell me what I want to hear. What. Are. You. Doing?"

His large hand gently cups my cheek, forcing my gaze to meet his patient eyes. For some reason that pisses me off. I don't deserve it. It can't be real.

"I'm not doing anything!" I shove his arm away from me. "I just…I need to be alone, I guess."

"Too bad. I'm coming in with you. You drank enough to give even *me* a buzz and you're a quarter of my size. Not to mention this has been an emotional night. You're not going in there alone to stew. I'll sit on the couch while you sleep if I have to, but I *am* coming in with you. End of fucking discussion."

"Okay, *daddy*. Whatever you say." Realizing this is definitely not a battle I'll win tonight, I concede with a roll of my eyes and turn, unlocking my front door.

His tone is doing things to my insides I would rather not feel, so my only line of defense now is my feisty retorts. The hard swat against my ass has me leaping through the door just as his harsh breath wafts past my earlobe, his chest pressed tight to my back as he speaks.

"I don't care if you're drunk or not—call me that again and I'll take you to bed and fuck the sass right out of you. Don't think I won't." My skin tingles.

I dash into my bathroom to change, almost tempted to take him up on the offer.

CHAPTER THIRTY-FOUR

PALMER

IT'S PUSHING MIDNIGHT AND MY eyes keep fluttering closed as I mindlessly flip through channels. The long, draining day is finally taking its toll, but I'm determined not to fall asleep without talking this through. Kennedy is silently reading next to me—has been for the past half hour—although *reading* is quite the stretch since she just looks lost in thought and the book itself is fucking upside down.

"Reading anything stimulating over there?" Using the back of my index finger, I brush away a strand of hair lying across her eye and lean in her direction. She noticeably shrinks back into the couch.

"Sure…everything is fine."

Okay, what the hell? Now she's not even listening to me.

If I didn't know this girl like the intricate linework on the back of my own hand by now, I'd probably chalk this evening's sour mood up to too many drinks working its way into a nasty hangover, but I know better than that. She flips another page. This girl is a damn terrible faker.

"Okay." *Deep breath.* "Should I be…worried?" I pause.

This grabs her attention. Her eyes shoot up to meet mine, darting back and forth, questioning my meaning.

"What?"

"*Worried*," I repeat deliberately slow. "About you, tonight... *us*? Most importantly, your ability to read." I flip the book in her hands, snapping it shut. "It's been upside down since you planted your ass on the couch," I bark. "Should I be worried about something other than the obvious?"

"No."

The pounding of my heart between my ears fills the silence in the room.

That's it? That's all the response I get? She can barely look at me.

I sigh as I stand from the couch and extend my hand down to her. "I'm tired. Let's just go to bed."

She stands, ignoring my outstretched hand, and the book she was 'reading' drops to the floor with a loud *thud*.

"I don't want to have sex. I'm on my period."

What? Okay...

"I don't mind sharing a bed with Aunt Flo."

Her eyes squint to thin lines and I drop my hand back to lie limp at my side.

"Kennedy, who the hell cares if you're on your period? I'm not trying to plow you in your current state. I said *go to bed*." I snarl. I can't help my voice from escalating, but she is seriously testing my patience tonight.

"I'm not in a giving mood, either." She drops her gaze to my crotch and back up, with her eyebrow raised and her lips pursed.

She rolls her eyes just as I narrow mine.

Deep breaths...three...two...

Nah.

"Are you *intentionally* trying to piss me off?" I growl, my eyes boring into hers, hoping beyond hope that the liquor she ingested earlier in the evening is pulling the strings attached to her fucking attitude. "I don't stick around for sex. I stick around because I fucking care about you."

"We sure do screw a lot for that to not be a factor in you being with me." Kennedy scoffs, prowling closer, and steps over the fallen paperback. A look I'm not familiar with spreads across her face.

"We do. I don't remember hearing you complain before now."

"Am I complaining?"

"No. You're pissing me off is what you're doing. I'd just like to know why."

Her small hand flattens against my ribs and she heaves her weight into me, my body falling to the couch below. Her thighs land to either side of my lap, trapping me against the cushions, her pussy pressed so hard against my groin I have to stifle a groan.

This is a test. I know it's a test, but the way she's bucking her hips, crushing herself down onto me…my resolve is crumbling. I'm putty in her hands, and said hands are working their way down to the drawstring of my pajama pants. Our panting breaths fill the room around us, drowning out the television.

"You've never raised your voice at me before. I think I kinda like it." She grinds her hips once more, rolling her head back and breathing out the sexiest moan. "Does this look like complaining?"

"I thought you were"—she grinds down harder against my screaming cock, just begging for release from the stifling fabric between us— *"on your period,"* I grate out.

"No." She continues her onslaught against my raging hard-on, clearly enjoying the hell out of this. I'm fairly sure she's having a break in psychosis, but I can't bring myself to push her away. Not now. "I just—I needed to know that you're in this for the right reasons, but right now I don't even care. I just want you inside me." A single tear falls, her finger swiping it away before I can be positive it was actually there. "*Please.* I just want to forget about tonight."

A good man would turn her down, put her to bed, and talk about this shit show tomorrow.

But I've told her before I'm not a good man.

My restraint is gone.

My willpower left in a puddle at the door when it comes to Kennedy Darling.

When I say nothing, her lips crash down onto mine, quieting the thoughts tumbling around in my damn head. The only thing I know for certain is that I need her and she needs me. Tasting her lips, her peach scent flooding my nostrils, the roll of her hips against mine; it's sensation overload. With a growl, I pull her body tight to mine, her soft breasts connecting with my hard chest.

"Please, Palmer. I. Need. You. Inside me." She kisses me between words, her needy plea music to my ears. With one quick tug, she pulls the front of my pants down, unleashing my rock-hard cock from its confines. It bobs between us, already the head glistens with pre-cum, begging for her hot center. My eyes stay glued between us as she slips aside her booty shorts, dropping herself down onto my length, completely devouring me to the hilt.

"*Fuuuuucking hell.*"

She begins bouncing up and down before I can even catch my breath from the initial shock of her descent on my jock. She tosses her head back, rolling it between her shoulders with her lip held prisoner between her teeth. I tear the shirt from her torso, her arms lifting as I peel it off, displaying those perfect tits. I suck a pebbled nub into my mouth as she continues to ride me. She squeals, steadying herself against my arms.

"That's right, baby. Use me. Let it all out." I grab onto her hip, marking her smooth skin with our encounter. "*Harder.*" Wrapping an arm around her back, I secure her to me and she picks up her pace. Her moans fill the room and I swear I grow even harder within her.

"Kiss me," she pleads.

I pull down on the back of her neck, joining our mouths as I snake my tongue between her lips, lapping up everything she's giving. I tug at her hair and she opens wider for me, our tongues tangling as I pummel in and out of her faster, meeting her thrusts with my own. Our bodies are frantic and relentless, but our kisses are intimate—wholly devouring each other.

"I can't get deep enough, I…fuck. I love you, Ken." I pant into her mouth. "I love you so goddamn much. I'll never stop."

The sound that escapes her lips sounds so much like a cry that I almost pause, but she tugs my hair by the roots and my mind short-circuits. Our bodies are melding, completely intertwined when her hand trails up my chest toward my throat, applying just the faintest bit of pressure on the sides, and fuck me if it isn't the hottest goddamn thing in the world. She's racing toward her own orgasm, taking from me everything I can give her in the moment and in her inebriated state, clearly willing to try something new. I've never once been choked by a woman, typically taking the more dominating role in the bedroom, but I'll be damned. I nearly spill into her at that moment. Laying my hand atop hers, I push down, applying even more pressure.

"*More*," I grate out.

My little vixen complies, one hand over my throat, the other on my bicep with her teeth sinking into my shoulder. My eyes roll back into my head, probably gone for all eternity. Too many sensations at once, and I'm lost. Lost in her, lost in us and at my breaking point.

She leans in, nipping at my earlobe, making me groan. "I think you like my hand wrapped around your throat, Colson."

I growl at her use of my full name. Grabbing her waist tight between my palms, I pull her down harder, reaching so deep I'm not sure where she ends and I begin.

"Come with me. I need it." She pants against my cheek, and I throw every ounce of energy I have left into my up thrusts, mercilessly pounding between her begging flesh. Kennedy screams, her nails dig into my arm so hard I *know* she's drawn blood. The thought alone is my undoing and I finish, lightheaded with her hand still wrapped around my throat. A few grunts leave my lips as I slam deliciously, furiously, and undoubtedly into the one woman who owns me completely.

Kennedy comes down from her high, in my arms, and we're both left panting, staring into one another. Unblinking.

She removes her tiny hand, oxygen pouring into my lungs as I feel our releases dripping out of her. The result of our passion mixes, with our love spilling, probably staining her damn couch. I chuckle to myself at the same time the bulldozer strikes—

I'm not wearing a fucking condom.

CHAPTER THIRTY-FIVE

Kennedy

SOMEONE SHOOT ME. PLEASE. ONE right between the eyes. Make it quick.

The countless drinks I tossed back last night pound away at my skull like Whack-a-mole—one of the handful of reasons I rarely drink—I get hungover easily. I also turn into a colossal bitch when there's more liquor coursing through my body than any other fluid, and most importantly, I do *not* want to be my mother.

I peel my eyes open, squinting against the streams of light sneaking through my blinds, illuminating the current destruction zone that is my room. My throat is dry and raw and my stomach churns angrily at me for betraying it and drinking my weight in alcohol. I can't even remember the last time I had that much to drink, and I know I made a fool of myself with Palmer. Bits from the previous night are a vague memory, like a movie you've seen before but only remember certain scenes. I know I said and did some messed up things, so facing him today should be interesting. I feel the cool emptiness beside me, so I know he's not lying next to me.

I groan as I roll to my side. Wiping the crusty bits from the corners of my eyes, I see a note on my bedside table along with two orange pills and a large glass of water.

Take these.
Hangover will be a killer (not unlike your breath this morning, yikes).
Had to stop by the shop. Be back later.
I love you.
– P

The corners of my mouth turn up in a smile, even faint laughter proving to be too painful for my throbbing cranium.

I sit up, tossing back the pills as I chase them down with the still cold glass of water. The liquid glides down my throat, soothing the rawness. My stomach growls in protest, probably needing some sustenance, but the thought of food right now makes me want to blow chunks.

Why do I feel like there's something important I'm supposed to be doing this morning?

I ponder this for a moment, coming up with nothing, and swing my legs out from under the warmth of my covers. I pad my way into the bathroom to shower the remnants of last night off my skin. A bath sounds heavenly, but a shower seems less time-consuming given my current state of wooziness.

I massage my purple peach shampoo into my scalp, working my fingertips around to soothe the headache lingering just behind my forehead. The soles of my feet are black—a result of dancing barefoot all evening. The filth and grime pool in a dark gray puddle at my feet, swirling down the drain along with my heartache caused by my mother.

I'm not sure if I'll ever stop being surprised by her disparage toward me, but I hope that day comes soon, if ever, since currently my heart feels trampled on. That, mixed with my hangover, is proving to be a lethal combo.

If I ever have children, I will never make them feel this low. My kids will know they're loved. They will know they're important, valued. My kids—

It hits me like a cartoon anvil—*kids*! Palmer didn't wear a condom last night. I knew I was forgetting something! I need to pick up the morning-after pill today. It's very unlike us to be irresponsible with the rubbers, but apparently, I was a little pushy last night. I groan, rinsing the suds from my tangled hair, and I step out of the shower. I brush my fingers through it, trying to somewhat tame the knotted mess I'm attempting to pass off as hair today. Huffing and accepting defeat, I toss it all up into a bun and dry off. I snag my phone from the sink and shoot a text off to Palmer.

Me: Just showered, and you'll be happy to know I also brushed my teeth. Minty fresh. Heading to the store to pick up Plan B then back here to sleep.

No one ever tells you how embarrassing it is to shop for the morning after pill. Every single person I pass is staring at me, their beady eyes perusing my current state: short, lime green spandex shorts, my black Edgar Allan 'Poe Some Sugar On Me' shirt, slip on sandals with socks, and wet, messy bun. I might as well have a flashing neon light above my head screaming *hot mess express!* I keep my sunglasses on while inside, hoping not to be seen as easily, though my inked extremities make that a bit more difficult. Finding the correct aisle is taking me much longer than I anticipated, but over my dead body will I be asking a sales associate for assistance with this.

Oh, hello, ma'am, could you please point me in the direction of emergency contraceptives? My boyfriend left his spunk in me last night and I'm only twenty-two. I'm not ready for children at this current point in time. Married? Oh, no, we only met this summer. Can you please help me put a stop to the potentially growing seed in my uterus?

I snort. Yeah, right. I'll lap this store eight hundred times before I ask for help. How fucking embarrassing. I snag a basket on my next lap around, deciding to fill it with other things to distract from the fact that I need to swallow a pill to ward off any mischievous sperms from doing the tango with one of my eggs. Some makeup wipes, a 'black ice' air freshener for my car, some sour patch kids, a mango Naked juice, Chapstick…*seriously where the hell is this damn pill?*

I round the corner, swinging the basket at my side, when I see my target in the form of a pale pink box. *Thank God.* My relief is fleeting as I take in fifty different versions of the same pill.

Still not asking for help. Nope. Not happening.

I decide on a version of the pill that claims to work the best, and bury it within my basket when a cackle sounds out mere feet from me. My grip on the handle loosens, nearly spilling the contents. My Ray-Ban-covered eyes meet striking blue ones from down aisle five.

You have to be kidding me. Of all the days…

"Good call. He definitely has some Olympic swimmers

down there." Amber steps closer, her heels thumping against the threadbare carpeting. Who the hell wears heels at nine on a Saturday morning? I may look like death warmed over, but at least I'm practical about it.

I shoot a questioning look her way. Playing dumb seems to be my best course of action.

"You. My husband—the baby maker. You're scouring the next choice section. I may not be a genius, but I'm not completely daft, either."

"Oh, Amber. Didn't recognize you." *Smooth.* "Uh, no, I'm actually just looking for...*ah*!" I snag the first thing my hand touches and toss it in my basket. Hemorrhoid cream.

This day just keeps getting fucking better.

"Right." Her arched brow mocks me, and I turn, wanting to flee the scene before I embarrass myself further. I'm almost to the checkout counter when her lanky fingers latch onto the plastic basket carrying my merchandise, halting my escape. I turn to find her wicked grin securely intact.

"We didn't get a chance to speak the last time I saw you. You ran out rather quickly. I'd like to sit down and...*talk*."

"There's nothing to talk about."

"Oh, I disagree. We have plenty to talk about."

"Such as?"

"You. Leaving town. Leaving him *alone*."

"Him? You'll have to be a *bit* more specific. Can't be too sure who you're referencing—I've heard you've made your rounds."

Her eyebrows rise, probably shocked that I'm coming out of the gates swinging, but my head is throbbing and the last thing I want to deal with is a psycho ex. I've had my fair share of those recently.

"I can tell you right now that I'm here to stay when it

comes to Palmer, so you can save your spiel for someone who actually gives a shit."

"Well, well, well. She speaks *and* she's sassy. I guess I really shouldn't be surprised. Colson always did like his girls a little on the bitchy side." She sneers, baring her perfect teeth. Just another reason to hate her—she's annoyingly beautiful.

I sigh. "Is there a reason you're confronting me first thing in the morning, in a CVS of all places? Need to meet a monthly quota or something?"

"I'm just trying to save you the heartbreak, sweetie. Colson will get tired of being with someone so much younger than he is. You are both at completely different places in your lives. Not to mention you'll be dating someone in their mid-forties before you even hit the big thirty. You're in your prime and not…*completely* unpleasant looking." Her eyes scrutinize me up and down.

Shove her face into the countertop—it'll look like an accident. "Sorry, Officer, she tripped."

"Do yourself a favor, *Kendall*, and chalk this up to a fun summer fling and part ways before he leaves you for someone his own age."

Oh, cute, the whole wrong name charade. How fucking original.

"And let me guess, you're hoping that someone might be you?" Her petulant grin answers that question. "Why don't you do us *both* a favor? Let's not pretend you give a damn about my well-being." I place the basket containing my magic pill at my feet and cross my arms over my chest. "The two people who need to be concerned with the age gap are *Palmer* and me, and we could not possibly care less about that than we do."

"How nice."

"Isn't it though? Now, if you don't mind, we had a long

day yesterday, followed by an even *longer* night, if you catch my drift. I'd like to get back to my boyfriend and get some sleep."

Her jaw twitches in annoyance.

"Ah, yes…lack of sleep will take a toll on the human body. It's no wonder you're looking so wretched."

I grate out the cheeriest smile my facial muscles will allow.

Fucking bitch.

"When you finally realize your scare tactics won't work, that I'm not going anywhere, and see that Palmer is actually happy, I'll expect some sort of a parting gift…preferably in the form of cake delivered to *our* front door. Jealousy isn't very becoming on you; makes you appear even older. Palmer has moved on. You should consider doing the same, *Angela*."

Yeah, so I feel like being petty too. Sue me.

I drop my sunglasses back in place and turn to leave, tossing one more request over my shoulder as I retreat. "I'll be waiting—and I like vanilla!"

"I'm just sure you do," she grates. "Well it will be a damn long wait!"

I flip her off as I stroll out the automatic doors, forgetting what I came here for, buried in the basket, right where I left it on the floor.

CHAPTER THIRTY-SIX

PALMER

"BUMPED INTO A CRAZY WOMAN at the store claiming to be your wife."

Kennedy strolls through the front door of her apartment, dropping her keys and cell onto the catchall. She strolls over to where I'm seated at her breakfast bar, securing herself between my thighs and leaning with a huff against my chest.

"Great. I was hoping she would have left by now." I run my fingers through my freshly washed hair, even the mention of Amber causing the start of a headache to emerge. "Did she say anything to you?" At my question, Kennedy leans back looking guilty.

"Oh, she had plenty to say. We…talked for a minute."

I raise my eyebrows for her to continue. When she doesn't, I push further.

"The two of you talked? About what? Your shared terrible taste in men?"

She flicks my ear. "Yep, and I'll tell you all about it in bed. I need to be horizontal. Like now. I feel like I got hit by a truck."

She takes a few steps back, tugging on my hand to follow along. I take the opportunity to scoop her into my arms and carry her. She whoops once she's airborne, wrapping her toned arms around my neck.

I stroll into the bedroom and place her gently onto the wrinkled bedspread. Her body disappears into the sheets as she burrows deeper below the covers, pulling the top sheet up to her neck like a human burrito.

My human burrito.

Before I slide into the other side, I draw the curtains, dimming the room enough that it feels less like early morning, allowing her to rest.

"I'm sorry for yesterday...and last night." Her small voice is muffled, hidden behind her duvet. I tug it from her grasp as I slink beneath the covers, pulling her body flush against mine. She lays her head against my chest, her palm flat against my heart, and her tiny, soft body curves alongside my large, hard frame.

"You sure as shit can put some away. If it wasn't under such bad circumstances, I'd be damn impressed." I kiss her temple, drawing lazy circles along her back with the tip of my thumb. "Not to mention those dance moves...if I didn't already get hard just by looking at you, your cha cha slide would sure get the job done."

Her body shakes as she laughs beside me and swats playfully at my chest.

"Ha. Ha. I'm being serious. I was a mess, and I'm sure I did some things and said some things that were messed up. Thankfully, I don't remember most of the night, but I know I can be a tad...*bitchy* when I drink." She tips her head to look at me, just as I tilt my head toward hers. The sincerity in her eyes squeezes my heart within my chest and I brush my free hand along her temple. I don't plan to mention just how much she riled me up last night. No need to add insult to injury.

"You were fine." *Lie.* "Nothing I can't handle, and I certainly wouldn't mind inebriated Kennedy to come back out in the bedroom—she's a freak." I run my tongue along the front of my top teeth, chuckling as she shakes her head.

"Maybe she'll make an appearance if you ask nicely." The playfulness in her tone turns to a squeal as I roll her body over, pinning her to the mattress, only holding my torso up by my elbows.

"I won't ask." I run my tongue up the side of her neck, the slightly salty tang teasing my taste buds, causing her hips to flex, pushing up into my semi. "I'm gonna coax her out."

"Oh, you will, huh?"

I grind myself into her, pressing the head of my cock just so against her clit that she shudders. I chuckle again, repeating the motion.

Reaching for the bedside table, I snag a rubber and tear the foil packet with my teeth. "I think we both know I will."

And I did.

CHAPTER THIRTY-SEVEN

Kennedy

SO MUCH FOR COMING BACK to sleep.

I lie against Palmer's warm chest, the slow rise and fall soothing my aching head like the ebb and flow of the ocean tide rolling in. He took me three times since I got back. Each time equally as passionate and commanding as the one before it. My body sags against his, completely spent even though he did most of the work.

Okay, *all* the work.

That must be why his deep breathing has evened out—he passed out on me.

My stomach growls between us, and I rub my palm along my gurgling abdomen. I still haven't eaten anything today. Looking toward the digital clock to my right, seeing that it's close to dinner time, I'm torn between staying tucked into Palmer's side or getting some food.

My stomach screams at me again, making the decision for me. Slithering my way out of Palmer's grasp, I try not to wake him as I stand from the bed. His hand stretches out, feeling along my empty sheets, reaching for me even in his sleep.

I turn the fan on for some background noise to keep him asleep as I slip out the door and head toward the kitchen to whip up something for us to eat.

When I pull open the refrigerator, and then my pantry, I'm not shocked to find them both bare. Spending nearly every night at Palmer's, I haven't had to go grocery shopping for a few weeks. Ketchup, lemons, pickles in the fridge. Tortilla chips, garlic, and cookie mix in the pantry.

Nope.

Chinese food it is.

I dial the number for our food and begin picking up the mess that is my living room—discarded clothes, makeup, and our shoes are strewn about. As I'm about to choose a movie for us to watch with dinner, my bedroom door opens and Palmer's bare feet pad down the hallway. He's shirtless, and his inked chest and arms, rippled abdomen, and bed hair have my face locked in a permanent heart-eyed-emoji state of being. He rubs his eyes with the heels of his hands as he makes his way toward me.

"How the hell am I the one who passed out? I'm not even hungover." He wraps his arms around my shoulders, yawning and swaying me to a silent beat.

"Babysitting the drunk girl is a tough gig—you needed sleep too." I press my lips to his chest, breathing in his musky scent, so perfectly him. "I ordered us some Chinese. It should be here soon."

"Mmm, first your pussy now some cat. I'm sampling the whole feline family tonight."

Laughing, I pull away, pushing against his chest.

"You're so weird."

"Normal is grossly overrated, babe."

My stomach gurgles between us, just as the bell rings

and the angry creature within my stomach does a happy dance. I pay for our food, setting the giant brown bag of goodies on the kitchen island. I pull out the sesame chicken, fried rice, crab rangoon, teriyaki sticks, spring rolls, and beef and broccoli, along with two small slices of cake.

"Jesus, we feeding the whole neighborhood or what?" His eyes widen as he sneaks out a piece of chicken, popping it into his mouth as he seats himself on a stool. He moans around his fingers, pulling them from his mouth. I have to clench my legs together, simply the noise alone moistening the valley between my thighs.

"It's hangover food—I'm hungover." I shrug. "Plus, you eat enough for five people, so I had to stock up."

I take the seat across from him and we both dig in.

A closed mouth gathers no feet. We both erupt into laughter.

"What the hell does that even mean?" I'm keeled over as we read all of the fortunes that came with our meal. We have a ton in our possession since they probably assumed we were feeding an army with our massive food order.

"I have no idea." I giggle. "Hold on, let me read another one."

All your hard work will soon pay off.

"Ooh, I like mine!" I squeal.

"Why do you keep getting the good ones? Gimme another." He tears into the wrapper, demolishing his cookie against the table, and plucks the small white paper from the ruins.

Do not make extra work for yourself.

"That's not much of a fortune." I say.

"The fortune cookie gods are telling me to pull back on my tongue game—that shit is tiring." He smirks at me from across the tabletop.

"No problem. I have my trusty bullet and plenty of double As. Buzz has seen me through some lonely nights alone this summer so far, anyway. At least he's up for the challenge." I shrug, hopping down off the stool to grab a glass of water. The food definitely hit the spot. I practically licked my damn plate clean before Palmer even made a dent in his. I smirk to myself, my back facing his direction, waiting for his next words.

"Oh, I'm up for any challenge when it comes to you, Darling. Way up."

When I turn, his gaze is hot, lingering, and all but devouring me from where he sits across the room.

I shrug. "I don't know…seems kinda like it's too much work for you. Buzz never complains…"

"Are you honestly telling me about you masturbating right now and not giving me a play-by-play or live action demonstration?"

I give him a teasing smile and nod.

Before I can stop it, I'm over Palmer's shoulder facing the ground, his large hand clapped over my ass to keep me from toppling over.

"Enough of that. Time for dessert."

Palmer's long legs bound toward my bedroom, pulling a belly rumbling laugh from within me as I slap at his back.

"You haven't even finished dinner yet!" I screech.

"Fuck dinner, I'll eat you instead."

I squeal as he tosses me like a rag doll onto the bed,

tearing my panties down my legs in one fluid motion.

Palmer suits up, enters me and I am whole.

The first thrust is usually a shock to my system—a foreign, very large, very thick, very *perfect* intruder. My entire body reacts with the slightest pinch of sweet, delectable pain, followed by a ripple of heat along every inch of my skin.

It's like this every time, and I know he feels the same connection too. He trembles slightly above me as he works his way into me, fully secured inside right where he belongs.

"It's just you and me, baby. All we need." He pants against my skin. "We stick together and everything will be just fine."

It's a promise after the last few weeks full of twists and turns. I believe it too.

Turns out…we were fools.

CHAPTER THIRTY-EIGHT

Kennedy

THE PROBLEM WITH THE WAY of the world is that when you're miserable and sad, lonely and depressed—the days drag like a limp leg behind you, painstakingly slow. On the other hand, when you're having fun and enjoying life—the days seem to fly by. My experience is no different. It's been nearly six weeks since the wedding, with all the days since blurring together when I only want them to slow down.

My mother has been MIA since the showdown at the wedding. Jim spoke with her once she stormed off, telling her she was no longer welcome to come around until she got her shit together or apologized to me. I won't be holding my breath for either.

Jason Laurent hasn't shown his face since my creepy run-in with him at the bookstore, which I for one, am thankful for. The guy gave me the damn heebie-jeebies. Palmer's more worried that he hasn't shown his face, afraid Jason is cooking something up in true Laurent fashion. The whole *no news is good news* saying doesn't quite apply when it comes to shady characters.

Rumor has it, speaking of shady, that Spencer left town to stay with his mother in Portland. Once his court dealings were over, that is. I decided not to press charges against him, only wanting to completely disconnect and not drag out a trial and put yet another target on my back. It was required through the state of New York, however, that he receive mandatory rehabilitation treatment. Supposedly, there was enough cocaine coursing through his system the night of the party to put even the biggest of coke heads out of commission.

Palmer and I have never been better. I still have my apartment, but most of my belongings are moved into the house. It didn't make much sense to either of us for the continued back and forth when I spent nearly every waking moment at his house anyway. We don't get stared at when we're out together any longer. We're just your average run of the mill couple. It's taken a lot to get here, but I wouldn't have changed a thing.

Well, okay, maybe a few things…

Our lives have been normal and comfortably slow since the night of the wedding.

Little did I know the wedding fiasco would be the least of our worries.

There's a saying that bad things come in threes; you know the one. What they don't tell you is red flags also come in threes.

In the mail this morning, we found an invite to a soft opening of a new restaurant in town; *Cabella*. Neither of us knows who the owner is, and we were both slightly shocked to find it addressed to Palmer and myself. No one knew we were living together. Red flag number one.

Not one to turn down food, Palmer suggested we go.

What could go wrong, right?

The food is *delicious*. Choosing crispy Brussel sprouts with bacon and maple butter glaze as an appetizer, we test the waters. I practically orgasm on the spot. Palmer selects the scallops and a whiskey neat while I opt for the peanut Thai salad with grilled chicken and a glass of water. I haven't had a drop of alcohol since the night of the wedding—the world saw enough of Train Wreck Kennedy that night to last a lifetime.

With dinner going so well, we let some of our unease go at the oddity of the invitation. The fact that we don't know a *single* person in a town as small as Beacon Hill should be a good indicator to get the hell out while we can. Red flag number two.

Palmer excuses himself to use the bathroom, his stomach not quite settling well, and I wander about, admiring the design of the place as well as the artwork on the walls. Fifteen minutes or so pass, and there's still no sign of Palmer. I decide to go in search of my date. Red flag number three.

The trifecta.

I open doors, check the bathrooms, and at a loss for where he might be, step outside for some fresh air off the back porch. The deck overlooks a sun-kissed skyline, and there, standing at the terrace below me is Palmer.

With Amber.

Out in the open. Without trying to hide it. Without *me.*

I have a perfect view of their conversation from where I stand, the angle of the porch keeping me hidden from their view. Her long bob shines and her ruby red dress hugs every curve just so. She takes a step toward him. He doesn't take one back. I stand, my mouth agape as I watch the exchange before me unfold. Neither of them speaks, which somehow makes it all that much worse—the talking is being done through their eyes.

I continue watching. I couldn't move even if I wanted to. I watch, enraptured, as Amber rises to her tiptoes, cupping Palmer's cheek within her ruby red claws, right before she presses her lips ever so gently to his. Bile climbs up my throat and I throw a hand over my mouth to contain the sob that threatens to spill out.

Somehow, the Earth doesn't collapse. The world keeps spinning, although my world systematically changes forever in that moment.

One.

Two.

Three.

Four.

Four damn seconds.

It takes *four* fucking seconds for him to pull back. Four of the longest seconds of my twenty-two years on this planet. Her eyes look hungry, while his are hooded—almost angry. He knows nothing about anger. What I feel at this moment? *That* is fucking anger.

How could he do this to me?

Why her? After everything he told me.

Palmer takes a step back then, as she takes one forward. I peel my eyes away, unable to watch their little dance any longer. The squeak of the wooden floorboard beneath my feet causes them to look up at that very moment.

Shit.

Palmer's eyes widen—the shock, dread, and regret that

shine back is new. Utter horror begins completely taking over his gorgeous features I've grown so in love with.

"*Fuck*. Baby, no. Wait!"

He bolts inside to find me and *explain*, I imagine. Amber stays rooted in place, her disapproving eyes scanning over my body like one would assess dirt coating a newly polished floor.

I race as fast as my short legs will take me, straight to the bathroom to throw up the misery churning inside my gut. I find it odd, me throwing up. I've never done that before in response to something like this.

Then again, my world had only ever been this shattered once before.

Colby.

I curse myself for even thinking of comparing the two situations.

I wipe at my mouth, dabbing the corners with a paper towel as my ghostly reflection peers back at me. Pushing off the sink, I exit the bathroom, bumping straight into a very tall, hard, and rigid frame.

"Oh! I'm so sorry, I—" Cobalt eyes peer down at my tear-soaked ones, cutting off my voice.

"You weren't the only one to catch that show, my dear." Jason Laurent tsks, shaking his head. "How could he do that to you? After *everything*?" His forced pout laced with fake concern toward my predicament only adds fuel to the growing fire inside. His words mirror the thoughts that bounce around my head, but even still, the fact that it's *him* saying them makes me want to jump to Palmer's defense.

For what? He fucked up. Don't defend him.

"I-I need to…go." I push past him, our arms brushing as I head toward the back door.

"I'm so glad you got my invitation, Kennedy."

My neck hair bristles at attention, gooseflesh breaking out along my entire body. *Of course* he had something to do with this, bringing us all here under one roof. I wouldn't be surprised if Spencer rounded the corner at this very moment finishing off this damn reunion.

"But who could possibly have anticipated that the evening would be so eventful?" His smug smile mocks me in my misery.

I can't stand here a moment longer. I will the floor to open up and swallow me whole—but the relief never comes. I exit out the back door, hiding amongst the trash receptacles in case Palmer comes looking for me—and of course he would. We practically lived together now. He was my ride here, for crying out loud.

I text Sterling to see if I can come over and if she could pick me up something at the store. I give her a one-item list—her shock apparent while she gives me the okay to head to her apartment.

I can still feel Palmer on my skin as I ride in the backseat of the Honda Fit, Halsey's raspy vocals serenading me all the way to Sterling's apartment across town. She is waiting for me when the Uber pulls up. My back pocket vibrates with a series of incoming texts just as I arrive.

Palmer: Where are you?
Palmer: I can explain!
Palmer: Kennedy, please don't do this.
Palmer: Goddamn it, please, baby.

Ignoring the messages and pocketing my phone, I sulk my way up the steps, right before Sterling pulls me into the biggest hug, unleashing all my unshed tears.

Even just days ago, I remember thinking life could not possibly get any better than this. Two of the biggest problems in my life were solved, Palmer and I were good, and now here I am hiding out in Sterling's bathroom, throwing up the contents of what was left of my dinner.

For the third time since I arrived in Beacon Hill at the beginning of the summer, I'm a stupid girl.

My whole world is about to go down in flames and I hold the match.

The two prominent blue lines on the pregnancy test in my hand solidify that fact.

TO BE CONTINUED

Interested in the continuation of
Kennedy and Palmers story?

Be on the lookout for book two,
available in 2020!

AFTERTHOUGHTS

The idea for The Way We Burn started for me during an English course at Plymouth State University almost ten (yikes) years ago. At that time, it was just a sample chapter to do for homework, focusing mostly on character development and dialogue. On that day, Palmer was born. Throughout the years when I would pick this project up, poke, prod, and tweak little bits and pieces, one aspect always stayed the same. *Palmer*. I've spent so much time on this piece that some days I forget he isn't a real person. So huge shout out to my freshman lit teacher who told me my dialogue was authentic: you pushed me to keep writing.

Music is such a huge part of my life, and really inspires me to create new content. A song can shape a mood, set a scene, and elevate a scenario. I tried to encompass that with the playlist of songs chosen specifically for this book. Kennedy and Palmer's story can be better understood by mixing music with the words—so grab some headphones and listen along. I hope you enjoy!

ACKNOWLEDGEMENTS

I mostly want to thank everyone and anyone who has seen or heard me blabbing about this project for months and months on end (and keeping the details top secret, at that). To my family and friends—and many strangers, via social media—thank you for letting me talk endlessly about something I'm passionate about. Thank you for allowing it to excite you as well.

To Victoria, thank you so much for being my beta reader and soundboard on more than one occasion. I knew with our similar tastes and your say it like it is attitude I could count on you to give me the feedback I needed, and you didn't disappoint. Your excitement to get new chapters from me really lit a fire under my ass (that's the way *I* burn) and got me excited to create more content. I am so grateful for you.

To my brother, Aaron, for assisting with the promotional material—your continued support in everything I do, and have ever done, means the world to me. I'm holding you to it that this will be the first book that you read fully (maybe just skip over the explicit scenes, yeah? Cause #Awkward). I love you. Always.

To Emily Lawrence, the editor of TWWB; thank you. Thank you for bringing
to light a touchy subject that has since been cut from the final product—I truly believe we made the right choice with that. You were so helpful, and any mistakes in this book (take it easy on me, folks) are mine and mine alone.

Najla and Nada Qamber, you are saints! To answering all five billion of my questions, to absolutely nailing the cover design and formatting—thank you, thank you, thank you. I quite literally could not have done this without you both. You each brought my vision to life and I'm still obsessing over the finished product. You are both truly amazing at what you do, and I'll be back for more books to come!

I am beyond excited for the continuation of this series, and I hope everyone else is as amped about it as I am. I know I left you all with a cliffhanger (I agree, they're the worst. I'm sorry! It had to happen!) but my hope is that you enjoyed this read and you'll want to follow along and see what transpires between Kennedy, Palmer and other characters in this series.

All of my love,
J.D.

ABOUT THE AUTHOR

Headshot by Éva Watson

Author J.D. Fondry has attended three universities, had six different majors (writing not included) and at one time had aspirations to be on The Real World, or The Bad Girls Club. She claims to be neither highly entertaining nor a bad girl, so both options were nixed.

J.D. currently resides in Vermont, the home of maple syrup, with her fiancé and three-legged dog, Harley. If she is not working on a new novel, she can most likely be found reading, binge watching Netflix, or stuffing her face. Most likely Mexican, as she is a serial taco killer.

She has a strange affinity for bleach blonde men, justifies her sassy attitude by simply stating she is a Scorpio, and hates the smell of flowers.

Her debut novel, *The Way We Burn,* is now available on Amazon and paperback.

STAY CONNECTED AND
UP TO DATE ON FUTURE BOOKS ON:

Facebook & Instagram: @J.D.Fondry

Made in the USA
Columbia, SC
23 April 2020